ISSUE 26: SEPTEMBER 2021

**Award-winning science fiction magazine
published in Scotland for the Universe.**

ISSN 2059-2590

Submissions of fiction, art, reviews, poetry, non-fiction are
welcomed: visit the website to find out how to submit.

www.shorelineofinfinity.com

Publisher
Shoreline of Infinity Publications / The New Curiosity Shop
Edinburgh
Scotland

140921

Cover art: Cameron Ax

Contents

Editorial Team

Guest Editor: Eris Young

Co-founder, Editor-in-Chief, Editor: Noel Chidwick

Co-founder: Mark Toner

Deputy Editor & Poetry Editor: Russell Jones

Reviews Editor: Samantha Dolan

Non-fiction Editor: Pippa Goldschmidt

Art Director (Acting): Caroline Grebbell

Copy-editors: Pippa Goldschmidt, Russell Jones, Iain Maloney, Eris Young

Proof Reader: Cat Hellisen

Fiction Consultant: Eric Brown

First Contact

www.shorelineofinfinity.com

contact@shorelineofinfinity.com

Twitter: @shoreinf

also Facebook and Instagram

Pull up a Log

Putting this issue together was a first for me. Not just editing a whole magazine, cover-to-cover, but reading and engaging with such a volume of work created by trans and nonbinary creators. It was like editing always is – fun, challenging, often frustrating – but the stakes were higher, somehow. The material closer to my heart. As I opened the first docx file to start reading slush, I realised I was nervous. In a way, I was putting my trust – tran to tran, as it were – in others from my community to bring me their best. I wanted to be proud, not only of my work as an editor, but of my community.

And I was not disappointed. The stories submitted were tender, funny, and nuanced portrayals of complex, flawed gender-diverse characters. While my guidelines said submissions need not feature trans and nonbinary protagonists, most did anyway – almost as if this was the mental default for the writers sending in their work! Not one of the stories I received objectified a trans character, no one was used as a plot device or killed off for shock value, or to fuel someone else's narrative arc. There was a deep ease in reading these stories – and poems, and in interviewing our featured author, KM Szpara – as if a barrier between myself and the work, that I hadn't even known was there, had been torn down.

The upshot was that I ended up with the impossible task of selecting the best of an excellent bunch. All I could do was go with my gut, letting my mood guide me. So the issue is as much a product of the talent and passion of the contributors and staff at *Shoreline* as it is a product of where my head was at while I was editing.

These stories spoke to me: B.G. Alder's *City of Corporate-Sanctioned Delights* features that rarely-seen beast: the nonbinary protagonist (two of them, even!) who's actually allowed to be disreputable, worldly and genuinely funny. Beth Martyn's *Trans Timelines* reminded me of another story, *Everquest* by Naomi Kanakia, published in Lightspeed Magazine. But while both contemplate the possible futures of a trans person who is unable to transition, and the way a person's life may be utterly transformed by a little kindness, by being nurtured and allowed to grow, Beth's story paints a more hopeful picture.

I gravitated towards quieter, more contemplative rather than action-packed pieces. The needs and wants of the characters, their interior journeys, are foremost, and the stakes, for the most part, are emotional. These are stories and poems of the quiet longing any person might feel--cis or trans, binary or not--for adventure, companionship, change, and the freedom and courage to be yourself. J Chng's narrator in *I Wish* longs for their lost forebears, while *Materials* by Harry Josephine Giles is an exuberant celebration of girlhood in all its forms. Without necessarily seeking them out, I've collected sparkling visions of trans, nonbinary and gender-nonconforming joy.

As such, working on this issue has been a joyful experience, and I hope reading it will be, too.

City of Corporate-Sanctioned Delights

B.G. Alder

W**hen Brick and I staggered** out of the atmo-entry taxi, my nostrils filled with the many odors of BLAM!™, City of Corporate-Sanctioned Delights. Fry grease and exhaust stink hovered over the crush of bodies. But I'd just spent eight consecutive weeks at the station, combing through algorithm-generated jokes and breathing my co-workers' recycled farts. I gulped down the fetid air of the docks like that shit was ambrosia.

BLAM!™ caters to people like Brick and me, working stiffs who get four days of shore leave at a time. While it's possible to go drink matcha lattes at a tidy Korean-style café, the dominant aesthetic is neon. They flash strobe lights in our faces until we keel over, stunned like city pigeons. Then they go through our pockets. Wherever we wake up, they tell us we got our money's worth.

As we plunged into the milling crowds, Brick was already looking wrecked. Their hair appeared electrocuted. Their pink crop top was stained with something I hoped was coffee. You'd dumped them over V-chat the night before.

"Hey," Brick shouted. The thump of bass was vibrating down to the roots of our teeth. "At least my big messy break-up came *before* shore leave."

I nodded, sweating. Obviously, this was not a good place to process one's feelings. But reading algorithm-generated sitcom gags all day will poison the brain. If the algorithm were writing this little outing to BLAM!™, Brick and I would get wasted on fruity cocktails, steal a parade float, crash it into a wall, fuck amidst the wreckage, and then get bailed out of jail by some repentant version of you, Brick's gorgeous ex. The conditioning had gone so far that a little goblin part of me actually wanted to do this, although Brick and I are good friends, and not each other's types.

Brick was already walking into a bar (there's a joke lurking there, but I'll leave it to the computers). Fake palms trees. Teal pools of vodka Jell-o, festooned with candy sharks. I watched Brick buy two very tall alcoholic slushies the color of spam and take them to go.

"I know you don't want to hear this," I said, as we elbowed our way down the boulevard, "but I don't think you should get wasted right now."

Brick took a long, noisy slurp from their drink.

"Brick, you said you loved her."

"Yeah, but what else am I going to do for four days?"

I didn't interpret this as a rhetorical question. We needed a distraction, an unsanctioned delight. But our seventy-hour work week had atrophied my creative and literal muscles. Brick and I are not inventors. We pick the rhinestones out of the shit.

"Let's do something the algorithm would never come up with," I said, aware of how lame this would sound.

To my surprise, Brick perked up.

"No alcoholic hijinks," I ruled. "No funky costumes. Minimal interpersonal drama. A weekend completely unfit for streaming."

"Okay," Brick said, with a glassy-eyed stare. "Let's go touch a cow."

"That sounds amazing," I said, mustering a ghastly grin. "Very tactile, very wacky. Definitely what I would like to be doing right now."

"Are you being sarcastic?"

I ignored them and started typing on my phone. Whatever happened, it was better than watching Brick slam down tequila shots with strangers. 'Cows blam (tm) where' generated a few commonly asked questions: 'What continent do cows come from? Are cows man made? Where can I tip cows?' More promisingly, I found a link to the only cow café in the city. I showed Brick the logo, a smiling cow offering up her own milk in a pitcher.

"Oh hell nah," Brick said. "I'm not drinking that bitch's juice. Look at her eyes."

Her eyes were, indeed, disconcertingly blank. But when I pulled up a digital map to the cow café and started walking, Brick followed me without question.

"Counter or booth?" the hostess asked, when we bumbled in, expecting – what, exactly, I wonder?

The café didn't smell of manure, or even warm hay. An espresso machine squealed. Buttery coffee smells wafted through the air. All the wait staff in sight wore head-to-toe cow suits, replete with pink silicone udders and polyester fur.

"Nope," Brick said, spinning on their heel.

I grabbed Brick's arm and hauled them back from the exit. Unlike most of the waiters, with their bovine fur-helmets, the hostess' primate face was visible under a fuzzy, black-and-white hood.

"Excuse me, citizen," I said, in my most adult voice. "Are you familiar with the award-winning, long-running situational comedy, 'Stuck in a Time Warp With You'?"

She licked her chapped lips and shot me a hard glance. Somewhere behind the mascara, I thought I saw a grudging glint of recognition.

"We are valued staff writers, here to conduct some research for a super-secret future story arc." I glanced at Brick, hoping for back-up, but they were busy stealing fistfuls of complimentary mints from an unguarded bowl. "Do you have, perhaps, a very small, non-human cow available for us to pet?"

With a single limp gesture, the hostess presented the costumed herd, the wall art above the red pleather booths, and the surprisingly banal-looking patrons. "We have many cows."

"Looks like a great place, but a little niche for our purposes." Out of the corner of my eye, I glimpsed a waiter squeezing synthetic half 'n' half out of his fake rubbery tit, straight into somebody's coffee cup. "What's this milk made of, anyway?"

She shrugged. "Lab-grown yeasts."

"Do you know where we can buy the real thing?"

The hostess' penciled-in eyebrows shot up. "You want to drink something that came out of a bio cow? Like, one that shits on the ground?"

"So what if we do?" Brick interjected, in a tone that worried me right away. They were crunching down free peppermints, not using their inside voice. "We want to feel something that isn't derived from petroleum. Eat something that isn't made from a chemical soup. We're tired of bull shit. The metaphorical kind."

Having made this speech, Brick met my gaze once and then looked away, plunging into moody silence.

"Ohh-kay," said the hostess, not quite rolling her eyes. "There is a high-end organic creamery on the edge of town. It's pricey, and you'll have to take the train. But I think they keep a few shitbeasts."

"Beautiful," I said, noting down the name.

A tablet glowed between the hostess' hands. When I gave it a tap with my phone, transferring a tip, it emitted a low, unmistakable moo.

Of course, there are a few public transit routes that can get you out of BLAM!™. But the city fathers made sure that trying to escape the municipal limits would be even more unpleasant and exhausting than staying put. After a bad, long wander, Brick and I found one of several obscure stops for the Green Line, a rickety train on stilts that is best known for having once unexpectedly caught fire.

The Green Train is forever flying the same route above the city, screeching and circling like a one-winged bird. When we rounded the top of the colossal staircase, the last passenger car was just rattling out of sight. We settled down to wait. In place of club music, distant taxi horns blared. Shreds of plastic bag blew and scuttled between the benches. If we'd still had trees, and seasons, they could've been autumn leaves.

We'd barely spoken since the cow café. Brick didn't seem tipsy anymore, just distant, watching pigeons with missing toes peck at crumbs around our feet.

"Do you really feel that way?" I asked. "About bull shit? Because it is our livelihood."

Brick peered up at the overcast sky. I followed their gaze, trying to see what they saw. Pollution, sure. But it was good to look at something other than ceiling – a clutter of brownish clouds, shifting with wind and heat.

"I was twenty-two years old before I learned that pineapples are real and blue raspberries are not," Brick said. "Some days I just want to knit, slowly. Get rained on. Put my hands in some dirt."

Ever since arriving fresh-faced at the orbital station of an entertainment giant to join a 'high-intensity work culture' and 'make the galaxy laugh,' Brick and I had bunked together. We'd eaten side-by-side in the mess every day. Although we'd seen each other's worst drafts, and bare butts, we seldom touched. I put a hand on their shoulder, feeling like a creep.

"Does this have anything to do with Selena?"

"It's the long-distance thing." Brick's eyes were wet, although mostly they sounded angry. "I have to stay on a company rig. It's in the fucking contract. They charge me for my room, they charge me for my meals, they charge for transportation. Three years and somehow I'm still in the red?"

Some social scientist must have observed the optimal time range for platonic touch, but I hadn't thought to comb through the research. Now I removed my hand from Brick's upper arm, worried I'd done it wrong.

"I'll never start a farm," Brick said, burying their head in their hands. "I'll never even have a container garden. What's the point?"

Our job may be degrading, but there is a kind of glamor to it. We live in space. We write TV. The algorithm does most of the work for our show and all the others; there aren't many human artists left anymore. But the chaos of mammalian humor eludes the usual formulas, enough to justify a few fleshy assistants. Brick and I had clawed our way into two of those slots, through means and methods I blush to recount. And we'd been paying for the privilege ever since.

I should admit that, unlike Brick, I wasn't wallowing in debt. My parents still wired me credits on birthdays and New Year's. Brick and I never talked about this difference between us. But then, I thought I knew how bad it was.

The Green Train came at last, bound for the outer districts. We found two hard-backed seats among the day-shift workers.

Around us, people in scrubs, sequins, and coveralls popped in their earbuds and let their faces go slack. Below the tracks, the blazing city slid by, shrieking for our attention. But I was looking at the deserted platforms, the weedy hell strips. Vines were snaking their way up through the cracks.

By the time the Green Train clattered to a halt, we weren't in BLAM!™ anymore. The commuters scattered, heads down. The air had gone blue and cool against my skin. I flapped my arms a few times, just feeling the breeze. There isn't night where I'm from – only a few hours when the sky goes pinkish gray.

Usually I navigated for us both. But Brick had already pulled out their phone and turned a corner. I stood at the mouth of the empty street, watching them go. Aside from the clean white glow of their phone, the place was dingy, scribbled with tags. Metal lattices shielded the windows. The shops and stalls were shuttered with corrugated steel. Up ahead, I even spotted an alley. They had alleys here, for God's sake.

"Wait," I hissed, my chest getting tight.

I wanted to warn Brick about muggers, and diseases, and logistical constraints. This seemed an unlikely place for a dairy. Even if it were here, it would be closed when we arrived. Soon the Green Line would stop running, and where the hell would we sleep?

But Brick was already disappearing into the dark. I sprinted after them, faster than I'd run in my whole noodly life. When I caught up, my heart pounding, Brick didn't even look up from their phone. On the screen, greasy with fingerprints, a blinking dot (us) was approaching a star.

The clustered buildings opened up into a long, wide, industrial street lined with warehouses. In the gaps between fluorescent lamps where the light began to dim, my adrenaline spiked. I imagined the sound of tailing footsteps. Then we came to the next lamp, and the brightness dulled my senses again.

Even here, the silence wasn't complete. I heard a high, electric hum; the distant roar of atmo-entry. My cheap jelly loafers blistered my toes. The last time I walked so far in one stretch, I'd been living planet-side in my parents' gated compound, where the fake lawns unfurled for empty acres and got shat on by tiny dogs.

"It's supposed to be here," Brick said at last, staring at a stretch of colossal unmarked fence.

I followed their gaze up, and up, and up. It looked like a border wall, spikes and barbs gleaming from its unfriendly top.

"It'll be electrified," I said. "They'll have cameras, and alarms—"

Brick put a finger to their lips. I listened, expecting the tread of a rent-a-cop, come to drag us back to wherever we were supposed to be. Instead, I heard a sound, starting low and rising into a reed-instrument moan. Another voice rumbled in answer, deeper and more insistent than the last. Unseen creatures shuffled and snorted in the dark. My synapses fired at random, trying to link the grunts and calls with something I could understand: circus elephants. Brachiosaurus herd. Bellowing humans. Whoever these guys were, they were tripping balls.

Something warm and damp brushed my hand. For an instant, I was paralyzed, wondering if I'd been licked. But it was only Brick reaching for me. We clutched each other and faced the forms looming out of the dusk. If it hadn't been for Brick's hand in mine, I would've turned tail. But Brick held me steady. Soon I couldn't look away.

The beasts trotting toward us were too huge, too rectangular, too quick to be cows. With them came a gust of warm, musky smell, not a sewage stink like I'd been led to believe. Strangest of all, every inch of them was in motion – round ears flicking, hairy tails swishing. Even their skins twitched. They crowded the other side of the gate and showed us their enormous white teeth, groaning and shouting, like we were supposed to understand.

There was no question – they'd made a bee line for Brick and me. And now, they were trying to tell us something. Their eyes were round and dark, fringed in thick lashes like a cartoon girl's.

"Are these cows?" whispered Brick.

"They must be genetic mods," I said, with a conviction I didn't feel. "Who the fuck would try to milk a thing like that?"

Whatever they were, they were still yelling. I glanced over my shoulder, dancing from one sore foot to the other. With all this noise, an authority was bound to find us. I didn't know which rule we were breaking, but I was convinced we'd done something wrong.

"They are," Brick was saying, with tears in their eyes. "They *are* cows. I love them. And look – they love me."

Before I could stop them, Brick thrust a hand between the thick metal bars of the gate. I watched, seized with envy and horror, as a thick primordial tongue emerged from one animal's mouth. In a single deft swipe, it slimed the salty knuckles of Brick's outstretched hand.

I am not proud to say this: I screamed. Brick screamed. In the shadows of the creamery, a gruff voice shouted, "Hey!"

Whoever it was, we did not stick around to find out. With their unslobbered hand, Brick was still holding mine. When they ran, I ran. My useless shoes tripped me. So I kicked them off. My soft, blistered soles slapped against the stinging asphalt. Pebbles and grit dug into my skin. But for the first time in my life, I felt fast, almost strong.

Beside me, Brick was gasping for breath. When we couldn't run anymore, we doubled over and wheezed. Nobody was after us. We heard no brachiosaurs over the buzz of the lights. When we finally looked up, we were laughing.

"The cow touched you," I said.

Every shore leave must come to an end. But this one, at least, we were going to remember. On the dawn of day four, Brick and I stepped into line with our co-workers, looking smug, well-rested, and bright-eyed. We'd spent the last two days of our freedom reconstructing our adventure in a 420-friendly hostel and watching archival footage of farms. For once, I wasn't concerned that Brick would throw up in the scanning chamber.

You don't need to be sober to pass an orbital re-entry check. You don't even technically need to be conscious. But when I stepped out of the sliding glass door, my body scan blinking red, a security officer pulled me aside. Brick was already waiting. They looked at me and shrugged.

A supervisor was called. When she arrived, she sat us down and cut to the chase. "Where did you go?"

"Nowhere, really," Brick said.

"Do you have any idea where you might've picked up a biological contaminant?"

"Nope."

The supervisor took us in with a long, slow blink. "You don't have any communicable disease, as far as we know. But there are traces of foreign matter that I can't classify. It's in your feet," she said, looking at me. "And on your pants," she said, to Brick.

I glanced sidelong at Brick. They mimed wiping off a spitty hand on their cargo shorts.

"I've ordered a fourteen-day quarantine before you enter the station," the supervisor told us briskly. "We're just playing it safe."

"That's great and all," said Brick, who'd actually read our contracts, "but we can't. We only had four days off, and we've used them."

"What about sick leave?"

"We're writers, man. You think we get benefits?"

The supervisor frowned, and held up a finger. "Let me make a quick call."

Several hours and one bureaucratic odyssey later, Brick and I found ourselves booted onto the street. More grateful writers with better hygiene would soon be imported from the surface. Our clothes and incidentals – one box each – would soon be rocketed down. As the last of our former colleagues boarded company taxis, we sat on the curb in high-UV sunshine, staring down the barrel of our new, untethered lives.

You don't know me, Selena, so I hope you'll forgive me for sending you this account. In a few days, I'll head home to the mansion basement, the disappointed parents, the novel no one will ever read. I will walk the tiny dog and sleep until noon. Brick is welcome there, on the downstairs couch. But the green grass is just baked sheets of astro-turf. You can't find dirt there. You can't even find rain.

I think you called Brick from your balcony once. You laughed at all their jokes, and sat in your own slice of warm, moving air. If you want to plant something there in the light, don't reply to this message. Write to Brick. And do it soon.

B.G. Alder (she/they) is a genderqueer, Seattle-based writer spoon-fed on Jewish folklore and Star Trek. A University of Montana MFA graduate, and Fulbright Creative Writing grantee, her work has appeared in *Jewish Quarterly*, *StoryQuarterly*, and the *Santa Fe Writers Project Quarterly*, and received the Amy Levy Short Story Prize.

In Search of Rust

Danielle Froom

He dreams of finding a great crashed hulk, a carrack or even a destroyer.

They're all gone, of course. Their league-long bulks; the bullheads and beams and coils, now nothing more than sod and wildflowers, earthworms tunneling where once electricity and plasma pulsed; the tall mounds where they'd crashed asunder or been laid to rest in neat rows were now good for nothing but picnics and sledding.

Every day after academy lets out, George combs the hills, knolls, and wide fields which encircle the city with open green.

Art: Cameron Ax

It seems to him that this is where his treasure should be, some bit of engine casing, a stabilization sensor, anything that escaped the reclamation teams and their microbial sprays – even just some stray ball joint or a bolt – damn, he'd kill for a bolt – but these are empty places. The transformation from works of art to works of nature is long past complete.

Knapsack sagging over one shoulder, he plods his way home as the October light grows dim, kicking over every stone and peeking into any groundrat burrow or muddy rivulet he might pass. On the last little knoll before the city's edge, Farran, Petal and the other pops are smoking organic spliffs from Petal's family farm. They mug and pose for pictures, Farran languorously circling them with his camera. George and Farran had been fast friends once – their great-grandmothers had fought together in the war, after all – but now they hardly speak. It was only a year ago they'd spent nearly every day together, but classes and interests waned, and a year is an incomprehensible chasm for fifteen-year-olds. From across the knoll, their eyes lock, then break away.

It will be weeks before even this modicum of interaction is matched. Another small eternity. He'd probably loved Farran, once, though he can't be sure. If it had happened, the last year had rotted the feeling and made it unknowable, like the sludge collected from every home's reclamator each week.

George hears them laugh as he turns away, and he tells himself that it's not him they're laughing at. And if it is, it doesn't bother him. He tells himself it doesn't *matter*. That he's better than them because he's no longer blinded by what *is*, with his eyes only on a horizon that's never reached. He's going to find something that *was*, and make it his own.

In rows where the wilderness ends and the city begins, and on every street corner and home, filmy solar fronds cast a faint glow over his trek, so thin they're only visible at the corner of one's eye. Even these fine pieces of old tech, one of the few holdovers from before the wars, draw George's ire. Would it be so bad to see them? To see the sun's rays captured, channeled and doled out? Must even this miracle be hidden?

He's heard of metal detectors; he's even seen old vids of them in action. Yet in many bleary hours searching all across the web, he cannot find a working model. There are replicas made from bio-plastics and used in period films, but he couldn't afford one even if he wanted the useless prop.

He's afforded a citizen's minimum, of course, but George's parents believe granting the full amount to children produces spoiled kids like Petal and his seven awful siblings. Thus, they hold back most of his monthly pay. On this one solitary thing, George agrees, though he'd love to have more credit like most of his classmates. A working metal detector would be otherwordly, but a chocolate soy cream at lunch would be pretty nice too.

At academy they speak with horror of the sky-high cities of old, the choked highways and poisoned rivers, the parched fields, the deserts on the march, and the vast dead zones over land and sea.

His history teacher waves his hands to furiously illustrate the mindboggling folly of machines which consumed the spoils of the earth and shat out poison in return.

His astronomy teacher rarely fills their days with the subject they ought to be learning, but instead with anecdotes from generations who never saw the sun nor stars, and who turned their gaze to the spoiled ground when the only shining objects in the sky were warships.

His science teacher shakes his head whenever George raises his hand, the man deriding all that came before them as simple antecedents at best. He calls plastics and alloys "monstrous bastards of man."

Everything is better now, they all agree. The teachers agree, his parents agree, his sister and her cadre agree, Farran and his former friends agree.

George doesn't want dead water or smog curfews or fracking famines. All he can think about is how his great-grandmothers' warships must have gleamed in the dark clouds and glistened in the hot rain, how their engines must have thrummed with a never-ending heartbeat of power, how the titanium and polycarbonates must have clanged beneath footfalls. He wonders just how tall the skyscrapers truly were – they're as mythical to him as whales were to his grandparents – and if it was true that the rich would throw coins from the top, wounding people in the street.

In his daydreams he hears the hum of lights and the rattle of air filtration, the thrum of high-rise trains and all the sound effects one finds only in period pieces and horror films.

The house is nigh-empty when he arrives, with his parents at work and Orchida at track practice. Their keeper putters around the living room; he always seems to be where George wants to be, and manages to reappear as soon as George relocates. George would prefer a robot, even if it were biologically printed. Their parents tell them – often – to be grateful, that *their* generation hadn't had a keeper for every home, but on this rare thing he and Orchida agree. Orchida says the keeper tries to read the messages on her tablet over her shoulder; they joke – their only joke, if they're honest – that the keeper is a spy.

George's assignments seem particularly designed to anger him tonight. He's in the upper academy now, and there's no more shirking the clear structure laid out in each piece of homework. A month in and his teachers already loathe him. He chugs through each essay, giving them the answers they want.

The tablet is so light in his hands it's barely there at all. Flexible, biodegradable, all-natural except for the most microscopic of wires and circuits. Were he to tear it apart, those strips of metal would dissolve between his fingers. Tearing it apart sounds wonderful.

Damn, he'd die for a bolt in his hands.

Winter has hit the province harder than expected this year. The academy has gone fully virtual a couple of times, adding to George's organic misery. At least on the walks to and from academy he can dream of stumbling upon great things. Trapped in this home printed from limpet hydrogels, even his daydreams fade.

Orchida's tablet rings out from dawn to dusk with messages and calls from her friends. Her fingers tap an unending silent beat on the tablet's soft surface. George's tablet only receives academy notices. Unsent messages pile up in his queue.

His father smells of the aquaponics barge when he sits down for dinner, and he seems happy with his new job. George is less sure; his father is never home, makes excuses about how important the new work is, and George doesn't like the reek. Every day his father tosses his work clothes into the household printer for cleaning and mending, but they still come out smelling the same. His father stinks like a field the morning after a night's hard rain. *Drowned.*

Over dinner, while Orchida moves the piles of poi and guinea on her plate into an illusion of consumption, George's parents quiz him on his week. His mother, too, has been increasingly buried by her projects, traveling to other provinces every other week.

"So good to be back in Burlington," she sighs every time she returns, long arcology designs rolled up in a satchel over her shoulder.

Burlington, George sneers inside. As if this low green place could compare to the old capital; George has seen it in history class. It was huge. It was beautiful.

They pepper him with questions. They ignore Orchida. Has he maintained his studies? Is he logging enough time on his tablet? Has he thought of rejoining the hybridization club? Why not another club? Petal and Scout are in three clubs, did he know that? They'd heard Candela's daughter Albany joined the geology club, did he know they're called rock hounds? Isn't that swell? And just whatever happened to Farran, did he know everyone, absolutely *everyone* thought they would've been a cute couple?

In bed, he taps the algae light above his head, knocking the verdant bits to wakefulness. Inside the water-filled tube the tiny creatures rouse in a quick tide, casting a soft glow over the room. It feels like he's sinking in a sludgy pond.

He knows of fluorescent and neon light, but films do them little justice. No matter how deep he searches on his tablet, the images of the old world do nothing to sate him. Yes, the streetlights are a hot yellow instead of pale green, but where is the brilliance? Where is the hum? The billboards blaze with life and scream to every passerby with furious sex and veiled insecurities. What a cacophonous world of urges it must have been, but he'll never know it.

His parents don't understand. Their grandparents told them of the days when the earth itself was rotten, when sickening smog rolled over towns and valleys, when even the richest cities had begun to corrode and collapse, when you could never even touch a river, let alone drink from it.

His parents loved to tell the story of how they'd seen the last of the girders go to bloom on their honeymoon in the remnants of New York, and he wished he could have been there. Just to catch that final glimpse of steel.

On the last day of school before springtide break, the bone bell dully tolling, Farran approaches George on the outskirts of the academy grounds.

Their school-issued knapsacks match, but everything else has gone cross-kilter in the last year. Farran has grown broader, his hair short in the back in the latest style, his clothes and boots the brightest cashmere Burlington's downtown has to offer. George may not have actually shrank in the last year, but he's never felt smaller than this moment.

Farran asks him to follow, but spends more breath on his spliff than on words. George has a sick feeling that he's about to get pummeled in the woods, like what happened to that kid with three parents in Middlebury Commune last summer, but he's pretty certain Farran wouldn't do that. Petal might.

Instead of the woods, Farran leads him around the knolls outside the city proper and down to the aqueduct, carved from flowstone onyx to provide half the state with fresh water from the mountains – as if the crystal-clear canals running through the city could ever contain the slightest taint.

Farran leans against one of the aqueduct's massive pillars, lights another spliff, and runs his fingers over initials in the stonework. He offers George a puff and they pass the joint back and forth as they walk on. Like they used to.

"Came this way with Petal a couple weeks ago," says Farran. "His family has horses, you know. Lots. So, he takes us all out riding on the weekends."

George says nothing. He has nothing to say. Farran falls silent too, tossing the half-gone spliff into a puddle. His camera bounces at his hip with every step, but his days of waking the device for George are gone.

They follow the aqueduct for another two miles, then down an embankment into a mossy damp ditch. Under the blanket of green lies a slab of pale gray rock, but no god or planet put it there. George feels a lump in his throat. He wants to kiss Farran.

"Concrete?" asks his ex-friend, pronouncing each syllable like a separate word.

"Yes."

"You were always going on and on about it when we…" Farran falters. "When saw each other more."

George leaps into the ditch and savors the slap of his boots on the concrete. Kneeling, he rips up a clump of flowering moss to get to the beauty beneath. When he turns to thank Farran, he's gone, and only then does George realize some time has passed. The sun is lowering and he's already missed dinner. Missed a chance to say thank you.

He tears at the ground until the last rays of the red sun drain from the ditch. Fingers clutching, grasping and frozen, he clears an inch down and ten feet in either direction. It's a wall, a fallen structure. There has to be more to it.

Propping his cell against a pile of ravaged moss, he illuminates the area and scurries back to work. George hurls away tumbled stones and new shoots and creeping roots with bloodied knuckles. A gap in the concrete opens before him, maybe a window, maybe a way in. Yet as he plunges his hands past the gap, they go no further than a finger's length before scraping against another layer of concrete. George curses as the moon comes out overhead, working his way around the square, scooping out every last bit of loam and mud. His fingernail catches on something hard, unforgiving, and he swears in defeat until he sucks at his torn finger.

He's tasted blood, of course – what kid hasn't – yet he's also read that blood tastes *metallic*. And what meets his tongue is beyond that. He jumps to grab his cell, nearly drops it, catches the filmy rectangle and tells it to maximize its light. Where pink nail meets dark skin there are smears of a color more vibrant than any drop of blood.

A treasure slips loose from his excavation, a small wonder clasped in his numb, trembling hands. George staggers home with it, dazed in the dark.

His parents spend few words on where he's been. They hardly bother with the holiday comings and goings of George or his sister; aside from middling grades, their worst fears are that Orchida will lose her place on the track team or that George will break a leg on one of his wanderings. Orchida eyes him from above her tablet but says nothing. They hold firm to the cold war secrecy of siblings.

In his room, George searches for a space. He's never had a secret before. Not a physical one. Nothing *real*.

The room flows too well, from one object to another, every single bit connected without a care for the travails of teenagers. George slides his hands along the window ledges and corners of his closet, but everything was printed with precision. There are no gaps, nowhere to slip his brilliant gray treasure. His desk is a solid piece with no drawers. His dresser calls to him, but his parents still do his laundry, and there is nothing sacred when it comes to laundry. He clutches the bolt, so tight it bites into his palm, and he grins. He feels high.

The bed. He walks around its corners, smiling as he thinks of the slab of concrete in the woods. Kneeling on sore knees and ripped pants, he eyes the underside, but the clearance is too high. Yet by the head of the bed, where the mattress and the baseboard and the wall all meet, there lies a possibility. The bolt, two inches long and interlaid with black dirt and bright rust among streaks of aged brilliance, disappears into the crevice and George laughs at the wondrous secret he's made.

George lies on his bed, his head spinning. He rubs at the cut on his finger, mushing the flesh until it turns pink once more and the cut re-opens, ogling the golden orange where it mingles with his blood. He knows it's a bad idea – and wonders if his vaccines cover things which aren't supposed to exist anymore – but he waits until it congeals and opens it again.

They find the bolt.

It's mid-spring and George's treasure has gone orange all over, with only thin strips of its silver hue visible between the threads where he'd once attempted to clean it. Something in the air has gotten to it – poisoned it – and it's as obvious as if he'd painted a sign to its location. Ochre rot snakes from its hiding place, down the wall and onto the floor, a creeping betrayal. He'd known for weeks what was happening, but every time he took the bolt from its hiding place and despaired to find more of the metal wasted away, he simply tucked it back.

Their housekeeper discovered it on his weekly rounds, and George has never felt more like he's been spied on.

"Why would you bring this into our home?" his mother asks.

"It's just not safe, George," his father grumbles.

"Look what it did to the floor, George," his mother tuts.

Orchida scoops up her tablet and excuses herself from the house.

They feed the bolt to the biotic reclamator and George says nothing, nothing at all. In the green glow of the light above his bed, he rubs at the faded cut and cries himself to sleep in the middle of the day. He misses school.

His parents wake him for dinner, but as soon as he sees their concerned, pitying faces flanking his sister at the table, he flees the house and runs for blocks beneath the green glow of the solar fronds. He knows he has nowhere to go, no one to talk to, and realizes he left his cell at home for good measure. A horse whinnies on the outskirt of his neighborhood, cutting through a night with no sounds but the soft calls of spring frogs, and he wants to scream.

A street rover rumbles past, nearly knocking him over. It beeps a friendly warning, but it sounds like annoyance. George wants to kick it, though it's twenty feet away before he thinks on it. It greedily sucks up a Siryn coffee cup and straw which were already dissolving on the sidewalk, hours past their breakdown point. He wonders if he tackled the rover, if he'd find anything substantial inside. Would there be a hidden gem, some iron heart, deep within? Or would it too dissolve in his hands?

The solar fronds begin to dim and George realizes he's been sitting on the curb for some time. Across the street, a home identical to his own glows the same sickly green color within, silhouetting the family going through their nightly routine. One of the moms picks up a kid and spins them around until they nearly lose control, and all three of them laugh and spin together.

George knows his parents thought differently once. Even just a little. They gave him an *old* name, when all their classmates and colleagues, the children of the children of the last veterans of the last war, were naming their sons and daughters after nothing but flora and fauna. They named him after his great-grandfather, a civil engineer. They were born from women and men who'd built and lived in a different world, and they couldn't allow him a single piece of that world.

The night turns colder than any spring night ought to be and drives him homeward at last. He guesses by the nearly extinguished fronds that it's well past midnight, yet when he slinks into his house he finds Orchida still awake, tapping away on her tablet in their darkened living room.

"Where'd you go?" she asks.

He wills her not to speak. He doesn't want to talk to her, or worse, answer his parents' questions should Orchida wake them.

Kicking his shoes across the kitchen, he makes for his bedroom, but Orchida follows, the last lights of the day automatically dimming in her wake.

"Why don't you see Farran anymore?"

George shrugs.

"Was he your only friend?"

George groans, sliding through his bedroom door.

"Are you going to kill yourself?" she asks.

"What?" he snaps.

"Don't." She holds up the tablet to obscure her face. There might be tears there.

"Why would you say that? I'm not— "

"Just don't, George." She stalks down the hall to her own room, already firing away messages to her friends.

Her question felt like the punches he'd expected from Petal and the pops on that early spring day, a hundred years ago. Sitting on the edge of his bed, his eyes stray toward the spot where the bolt had lain in hiding, where his treasure had been buried. The stains are long gone.

From the end of the bed his cell chirrups. *Whatever you're looking for*, a text from Orchida reads, *don't die.*

He deletes her entire text chain.

An automated transport pulls up in front of their house just as George stumbles into the kitchen for breakfast, its egg-like curves shining painfully blue on this too-bright spring morning. George shades his eyes and glares at the pod through the kitchen window, dreading the import.

"Why'd you call a pod?" he asks his dad, slipping a pair of kelp slices into the toaster.

"Going to market," says his dad, finishing the last vestiges of his own breakfast. He pats his stomach. "Working on the agro-barge makes me think about food all the time. Should we get something special today?"

"We?" George asks around a mouthful of toast.

"We," says his dad. "You need to get out of the house. Late-night sojourns not included."

George eyes his room, wishing he'd stayed in bed. "I haven't been to the market since last summer." He thought of Petal's family and their market stand. Seeing him might make that stifled scream finally appear.

"Well, you're coming. I need help carrying everything."

"Get one of the restorative convicts to help you. I know they have them there."

"Rude," says his dad.

"What about Orchida?"

"She's at track practice already. Too busy, buck? If you have too much of a backlog on your tablet, you could go ahead and show me just how far behind—"

George follows his dad to the pod without another word.

The market is exactly as he remembers. Loud, smelly, and mostly uninteresting. Petal's family is there, the loudest of the bunch, hawking their marijuana and honey, but Petal is thankfully absent.

His dad haggles with a vendor over a bundle of rhubarb long enough for George to wander away. Past the market stalls, a collection of food pods and traveling peddlers have arrayed themselves in a semi-circle, in the center of which a group of kids from the academy are playing guitars and mandolins. George knows them all, but they trade nothing except the quickest of glances.

He idles around the half-circle, edging back before his dad whistles, then stops. Metal gleams in the spring sun. He crosses the distance in long strides, nearly dropping his dad's groceries. His hands shake.

The peddler has a pod opened to a smattering of admirers, jewelry glittering across a copse of plastic stands. His gems are fitted into bone or plastic and hung with hempen twine – yet a row in the back dazzles the customers, none more than George. He reaches to touch one, but falters as his eyes fall upon their prices. No one mines silver anymore. He doubts his parents could buy this man's wares if they saved up for a year.

George grits his teeth and steps backward, his eyes transfixed as he tries to turn away. It's just slivers of metal, he tells himself. It's nothing. Even his bolt was better. It *meant* something. His feet seem unwilling to move, and he tears his gaze from the jewelry, then pauses as one of the customers steps away.

Another display of jewelry rises to the right of the peddler's display, polished stones and translucent slices of red and blue and white, of golds and greens mixed in ways George has never seen before. It doesn't look natural. But it doesn't look man-made either.

"Are these fake?" George blurts.

"No, kid," says the peddler, laughing. "That's genuine fordite. Detroit agate."

The layers are gorgeous. "Detroit's gone," says George. "We learned about it at academy – it was the first great city to fall."

"That sounds right." The peddler shrugs. "Don't know about all that, just know what it is and where I gots it."

"It's a rock?" George feels like walking away.

"That there's the paint from the cars, you know about them, right? They still teach you about cars in school, right? They used to paint the cars all in a row, and the paint would just splatter all over the place. Millions of cars, millions, and all different colors." He snaps his fingers. "Cars go away, factories crumble, and all that paint just sits there a few hundred years."

George slides a pendant necklace from the display and cradles it in his palm. It feels like a stone, but its gleam is dulled, the colors dreamlike.

"Well, the earrings are a hundred-seventy-five each, the bracelets are two, that pendant there I could let go for maybe a hundred-fifty to the right customer." He smiles, but if fades when he sees George's face.

"I can't—" George starts, a lump in his throat and pain in his belly. "I can't afford that." He thinks of running with it, but puts it back on the table before the urge takes him. His feet are heavy and he wills them to move at last. George has never wanted to stay somewhere more. He's never wanted to run more.

"Hey, hang there," says the peddler. "Here, just a second." He rummages through a canvas bag on the side of his pod until he comes up with an object wrapped in thick cloth. "Ayuh, I knew there was one or two left."

In George's palm he places a thin semicircle slice of the same substance, the colors in lines instead of rings. He can almost see through it.

"Made a whole hell of those for jewelry and whatya, but a lot of 'em broke along the way. I'd let that piece go for, ah, seventy-five.

George places it back onto the man's cloth. "I've only got twenty credits."

"Hang there, here now, hold on." He snatches a different bag from his pod and comes up with an ugly chunk of rock, jagged and brown. Yet when he turns it to one side, George sees layers of color in its creases and crags. "Unpolished, unworked. You gotta do that yourself, so I'll call it twenty. Yeah?"

George stops at the threshold to his room and searches for some new secret place, but of course his room is less private now than it ever was.

Detroit agate, the peddler said. *I saw it when I was on my walk*, he rehearses in his mind, but that won't do. All it would take is an image search by his parents and the difference would be plain.

On his bed, turned away from the door, George wakes up his tablet and asks for pictures of natural agate. In its current form, the fordite is obviously something from the old world. He brings up pictures of agate jewelry, perusing hundreds before jumping up and out of the room.

The household printer takes some time to program, as if it cannot believe what its being asked to do. In the end, it acquiesces, and it thrums and clunks with the effort of cleaning and dividing the ore. George cries when it opens to reveal the results.

With three taps on his tablet, he joins the academy's geology club. He uploads pictures of the six divvied pieces of fordite for good measure. The club might know the difference. Maybe they never could.

Maybe it bridges the gap.

At academy the next day, he weaves his way through the student commons and finds Farran's workspace, relieved that neither he nor his friends are around.

He places one of the fordite pieces atop a pile of Farran's books and papers. What's left of the peddler's rock, polished and sliced by the printer, is thin enough to read through, with swirls of gold and black surrounded by red. The printer lasered a hole through the top, through which George wove a thread from his dad's sewing kit. The jewelry – necklace, suncatcher, art, whatever Farran might call it – is more fragile than anything he's ever held.

His stomach tells him to run, to rescind the gift. It's been too long. It might mean nothing to Farran.

The desk is ringed with printed pictures of Farran's new friends, a few of his family. And in the back, one of George. It was taken when they'd gone swimming at Mallet's Bay on Farran's twelfth birthday. George picks up the fordite and hangs it from the wooden tack holding the picture.

It might mean enough.

Danielle Froom is a writer of speculative fiction whose short stories and poems have appeared in *The MacGuffin*, *Blood Moon Rising Magazine*, *Disturbed Digest*, and *Atlas Obscura*. She currently lives in Buffalo, New York, with her wife and two wonderful, beastly children.

Trans Timelines

Beth Martyn

James looked up from his phone in shock as a loud, pulsating thrum filled his bedroom. A swirling mass of purple light had formed by his door and seemed to be growing larger and more defined as the seconds passed. He nervously cast about for anything he could use to defend himself, but only found pillows and a glass of water.

By this point, the energy had resolved into a portal about the height of a person. James caught a brief glimpse of a room full of complex, chrome-plated machinery before two women stepped through and the portal abruptly closed.

One woman was tall and thin, with cat-eye glasses and a lab coat over a band t-shirt, while the other was short, with a shock of blue hair, several piercings, and a denim jacket studded with pins. James held up his glass of water in what he hoped was

Art: Bestdesigns

a threatening manner, right before the taller woman started to laugh.

"Sam, I was telling you I got it to work! And oh my god, look at tiny egg me!"

The woman's voice was slightly deeper than James was expecting, but at least she didn't sound…threatening? And the more he looked, the more he had a vague nagging feeling that she looked familiar. A bit like his mom, actually, if you changed the hair color and added glasses.

Now focusing on James, the taller woman seemed to realize something. "Oh, I'm sorry, you're probably really freaked out right now. So basically, uh….I'm you from the future." She looked at the shorter woman again before the two of them broke into laughter.

"I … uhh … what the fuck? Is this some kind of prank? How did you make that thing appear, and how are you in my room? What the actual fuck is happening?!"

The taller woman finally steadied herself. "Sorry, sorry, I should explain better. I— So, basically I'm Jamie, this is my partner Sam, and I'm you from a decade in the future. Specifically, a version of you that transitioned and then, well, invented a working time machine." She shrugged.

"You're *such* a genius, babe," Sam chimed in, wrapping her arm around Jamie's lower back.

James squinted at Jamie. He couldn't deny that she looked related to him, and even had a similar face, although it was rounder and had generally softer features.

"Okay, I guess I believe you're from the future because I really don't have a better way of explaining that portal thing that you jumped out of. You're *me*, though? Like, I'm not a girl. I admit I read a lot of gender bender stuff online but it's not even that unusual a thing to be into for straight guys, and I've considered that I could be trans but there really just isn't a good reason to think that. I took a quiz that said I was a guy with some feminine tendencies and everything."

Jamie facepalmed. "God, I remember that fucking quiz. I don't know what dumbass thought they could make a multiple-choice survey that TELLS YOU YOUR GENDER. That's so fucking stupid." She suddenly perked up. "Oh, I have more evidence!" Jamie pulled out a phone, unfolded it into a tablet, and shoved the screen towards James.

James gingerly accepted it, seeing a series of photos that started with him, and slowly got more feminine until the last photo, which was clearly Jamie. "Wow, I, uh … that's … how did you do that? Is that deepfakes or something?"

She sighed. "Fair enough question. Here, I'll tell you something no one else would know. One time in sixth grade, during math class, you peed a little in your cargo shorts, enough that it was visible, but you got away with it and no one noticed because your shirt hung down so low that it covered it. You have a crush on Stacey Abrams, you have a birthmark shaped like Texas on the back of your left thigh, you have an idea for a super hero named Renderman who can temporarily make solid projections of digital 3D models whose power is only limited by the number of polygons, and your email password is LammaNinjaBanjo08.26."

James sat there for a moment, stunned by the torrent of private information, before handing the tablet back to Jamie. "I, uh … yeah, either you're psychic or … I guess you're telling the truth. W-why are you here, though? You didn't just come back here to show me some photos, right? Aren't you worried about causing a paradox or something?"

Jamie started to speak but was drowned out by another loud humming noise. Another portal – this time green — was opening near James' closet. After a few moments, a man wearing a lab coat stepped out and the portal closed.

The man also looked strangely familiar to James. In fact, he looked like a cross between old pictures he had seen of his grandpa and James himself.

Jamie swore quietly under her breath. "God, not this asshole."

The man strode over to James and grabbed him by his shoulders. "Listen to me, James. Do NOT believe anything these women say. They're trying to lead you down the wrong path. I know it may seem tempting, but if you reject their degeneracy, you'll come out the other side stronger, I promise. I should know; after all, I'm you from the future."

Jamie turned to James. "Unfortunately, this is also your future self. I met him when I visited your high school graduation while testing the time machine. Wish I could say we have nothing in common, but we at least both work in applied chronophysics and chose the same test location." Jamie was staring daggers at the man. "Fuck off, Jim. Take your weird alt-right bullshit back to your own timeline."

At this point, James was intensely confused. "I… I thought she was me from the future. How can you both be?"

Jamie started to talk before Jim talked louder over her. "So, the future isn't fully determined. You can think of it as a quantum event that hasn't yet been observed, so the superposition hasn't collapsed yet."

Seeing that James still looked confused, Jamie took over explaining. "Think of time as – a river. You and your present are in a boat that's constantly moving forward down the river. Up ahead the river splits into two branches. Depending on how you shift your weight in the boat, the boat could go down one path or the other. Both branches exist, but you and your present – the boat – can only take one of them. Maybe there are other parallel yous that go down the other branch, but you'll only experience one possibility. Like how a single Schrödinger's cat in a single universe ends up either alive or dead, but not both."

"Okay, I think I get it," James said. "So you could both be my future?"

"Yes," Jamie and Jim said at once, before glaring at each other.

Sam rubbed at Jamie's back. "Remember your breathing exercises."

Jamie squeezed her eyes shut and breathed in and out slowly, before seeming to calm down.

Jim, on the other hand, seemed angrier than ever. Jabbing his finger at Jamie, he started yelling. "Do you see this pervert? This half-and-half freak? You don't want to be like that, do you? Driving off everyone who loves you and cares about you, weirding out people on the street, destined to never have kids or a marriage or a stable job? Look, you're a good kid, right? You work hard, try to fulfill your obligations and avoid letting your family down. Imagine how they'd react to *this*. It would just be incredibly, deeply selfish to act on your basest impulses and to hurt your family like this."

Now it was Sam's turn to get angry. "Okay, shut the fuck up. You have no idea what you're talking about. First of all, Jamie is amazing and is dating me and has a great lab job, and she's closer to her mom and sisters than she ever was before transitioning. I'm not going to say people were great right away, but everyone who really matters came around and accepted her, and they can tell she's happier now."

Jamie hugged Sam, saying "You're amazing too," before turning to Jim. "Hey, how's your relationship with the fam? Oh, right, your anger issues meant you kept getting into fights with people about dumb shit and now half the family doesn't want to talk to you. And about no one loving you? Have you gotten around to dating anyone yet, ever, even though you're almost thirty?"

Jim briefly winced. "Okay, I'm saving myself for marriage, and I just need to meet the right woman. And besides, it's better to spend your vital energy on your career than it is to waste it on meaningless pleasure. Plus, I've gotten promoted more, and make more than you ever have."

Jim turned to James. "Look, even if you don't agree with what I said, you have to recognize the truth of what I'm saying. You took that quiz and saw what it said. It doesn't make any sense to believe your vague subjective feelings over objective, mathematical fact. And look, I'm not a transphobe, okay? I just think it's not the right decision for me – you – us. And you've seen documentaries and read stuff online. Real trans people know their gender from a young age, and there's nothing sexual about it. What you have is just a fetish, and although you might enjoy it as a fantasy, it doesn't make any sense to fuck up your real life and relationships by trying to chase some ridiculous dream. You've waited too long anyway, it's too late for you to ever become a convincing woman now that you've already gone through most of puberty."

Jamie interrupted. "That's such bullshit. I can't believe you've already given up on convincing her that she's not trans and you're just trying to scare her out of transitioning, so she can be a coward like you. Look at me. I look fine, I get gendered correctly pretty much 100% of the time, and unlike before, I actually feel like I look cute! And regardless of how you look, feeling good about yourself matters a lot more than what other people think."

Sam whispered "I think you look cute too," before briefly pecking Jamie on the lips.

Jim groaned. "Please don't rub your public displays of affection in our faces. At least not in front of the kid."

"Kid? She's a teenager. You remember as well as I do all the porn we'd watched by this age. Come on, if you're going to argue with me, you could at least not be so disingenuous about it."

Jamie dug around in the pocket of her lab coat before pulling out a bottle of pills. As she tried to hand it to James, Jim literally slapped it out of her hand.

"Okay, I've fucking had enough," Jamie snarled. "You wanna fight, douchebag?"

"Sure, I'll kick your ass if that's what you want. Show the kid how years of hormones degrade your muscles."

Jamie reached under her lab coat and pulled out some kind of streamlined, silvery gun. Leveling it at Jim, she muttered, "I was hoping I wouldn't have to use this."

Jim flinched backwards in shock. "Whoa, what the fuck?! You're going to *shoot* me? We were just having a civil debate, and here you have to go bringing violence into it."

Jamie turned to Sam before slowly lowering the gun. "Jesus, I wasn't actually going to shoot you. Don't act like you're the martyr here, you literally just assaulted me."

"Oh, come on, that was hardly assault. See, James, this is a great example of how this bitch stretches the truth."

"What the fu— You literally hit me! You hit that bottle out of my hand! Everyone here saw it. Why are you acting like that's fine and reasonable, but me just threatening you is a horrible crime?"

James decided it was about time to intervene. "Look, please don't hurt each other, okay? You're basically just hurting yourself. And besides, getting in a fight isn't going to do anything to convince me. I think I just need some time to think about this, okay? I'm not sure how time travel works, but could you leave now and maybe come back tomorrow?"

Jamie nodded. "Sure, I know this is a lot to process and you can take all the time you need. I'll come back the same time tomorrow – it'll only be a few seconds for me, though."

"And I'll also come back, to act as a counterweight to this bitch's lies."

With that, the room was suddenly filled with loud thrumming as both parties generated their portals and stepped through. James was all alone in his room, left in a sudden overwhelming silence to just lie on his bed and think.

As promised, they returned the next day at exactly the same time. Jamie popped out, alone this time, shortly followed by Jim.

"Hey, so hopefully you've had some time to think now. Have you come to any conclusions yet?" asked Jamie.

"Christ, stop pressuring him. Don't assume that all versions of us are like you."

"Please, you two, don't argue! You're just stressing me out and making it harder to think." James turned to Jamie. "So, I believe you when you say that you're trans and you're happy you transitioned. But it's not clear to me that that means *I'm* trans. What ultimately made you decide that you're trans?"

"Good question. So, I – we – used to think a lot about gender and I sometimes had this urge to try women's clothing or to try to look like a girl. I always suppressed those thoughts, up until I went to college, where a combination of new friends and the internet made me realize that cis guys don't constantly think about being girls, and that it was worth meaningfully investigating if I might be trans. I started out trying to wear women's clothing, and in some ways that felt better, but it also really forefronted all the parts of my body that I wasn't happy with. After thinking about things for a few months, I started the process to get on hormones. About six months after that I started to come out as trans to everyone, and about a year after that I also got around to changing my legal name. But basically, the key thing was realizing that you don't have to prove that you're trans. The very fact that you think so much about your gender means it's likely that you are trans. And I think it's just generally a positive thing to explore that and find out more about yourself and what makes you feel good, although it does take time to get past societal hangups and the feeling that you're doing something wrong or forbidden."

James nodded. "Okay, that's helpful, thanks. Jim, what makes you sure that you're not trans?"

"First of all, I don't like how you worded the question. It's ridiculous to ask me to prove that I'm normal. But in general, why *would* I think that? It's not like we grew up playing with Barbies or trying to wear dresses. I never thought I was a girl, and I didn't act feminine because I knew that just wasn't what boys did. Sure, like you two I did used to think about gender a lot, but I think I was just confused. Adolescence is a difficult time and our father has never really been around, so it's not surprising that I would latch onto my mother as the next best role model to emulate. And over time, I held strong and things have gotten better. I don't let myself dwell on gender or other unhealthy thoughts; instead, I try to focus on my hobbies, my career, and my relationships with others. Sure, being a girl used to sound nice, but realistically it's not an actual option. The most I could have been was a crude imitation of a girl, and to achieve that I'd have to be willing to sacrifice basically everything. Society doesn't really approve of people who aren't normal men and women, despite what some people might claim, and there's reasons for that. Humans evolved as men and women for a reason, so they could reproduce and raise a family in a stable unit. There isn't some magical soul or spirit separate from the body, and there isn't gender separate from sex. Thinking that you're another gender is a mental illness, indicative of something gone wrong in your childhood, and that shouldn't be catered to or it'll just get worse over time."

James scratched his head. "So, are you saying that trans people don't exist?"

"No, I just think a lot of people who claim to be trans have other mental illnesses. I'll admit there might be a few intersex people where their brain structure doesn't match their genitals, and in that case I support medical transition in order to have their body match their brains."

Jamie interrupted. "Okay, first of all, fuck you. People should have autonomy over their own bodies, and sex and gender aren't even close to that clear-cut anyway. Lots of cultures have had third genders, so don't act like our modern Western two-gender system is inherent and unchanging."

"Okay, look, I'm not saying that trans people or other genders don't exist. But the literature says that MTFs are generally motivated either by being aroused by the idea of themselves as a woman, or the desire to attract heterosexual men. In our case, with the amount of gender transformation fetish content we used to read, and frequent thoughts about how we'd look crossdressing, we're pretty clearly in the first category. It's called autogynephilia, and it undermines your dualist ideas of some gender identity separate from the body."

"I don't even believe in that dualist stuff, and honestly you're just trying to distract us from the actual issue. If you've actually read the literature you're citing, you'd know that even those authors are in agreement that transitioning is the ONLY successful treatment for negative emotions resulting from gender dysphoria. So the reason you want to transition is literally irrelevant. Besides, it doesn't matter if there's some definable, objective thing called gender identity. What matters is people doing what makes them happy."

Jim sighed. "Okay, you might have a point. But don't you think pursuing your own happiness at the expense of others is incredibly selfish? We'd all like to be happy, obviously, but not everyone gets that privilege."

"I just philosophically disagree with your way of seeing this. Someone transitioning doesn't inherently hurt *anyone*. Any negative repercussions from societal judgment are an issue with society, not something wrong with being trans. And it's not like being trans is a choice. The real choice is to suppress it and to deeply hurt yourself, or to express it and to be happy, but with some risk of others reacting badly."

"In an ideal world I'd agree with you, but we don't live in an ideal world. Someone choosing to transition knows what will happen, and acting like they don't is unproductive. You know our family lives in a somewhat conservative area and Mom constantly talks to neighbors and other parents. Do you really want all of them judging her as a failed parent?"

"I can tell you with certainty that that won't be what happens. Most people will be fine with it. They don't really care. Why should they? Most people are too busy worrying about their own life to really worry about others'. There are a few people who are rude and unpleasant about it, some awkward situations, but that's hardly the end of the world. Besides, most of those people were already not great, and I see this as just them revealing their true colors."

Jim rubbed his eyes. "Jesus, you just have a rebuttal for everything I say. I guess I shouldn't be too surprised, given that I'm sure you've thought about most of the same things, but I thought I'd have more rebuttals to you."

Jamie chuckled. "I'm not too surprised. I bet you haven't *let* yourself think about gender all that much, from what you were saying, so you're basically still in the same mindset as me several years ago. I think I've changed a lot and developed just from letting myself *be* myself, while you've been so tightly wound trying to be the person you think you have to be, that you've just ended up kind of running in the same place."

Jim sighed. "At this rate, you're gonna convince *me* that I should transition."

Jamie leaned over and hugged Jim. After a brief expression of shock, he relaxed and returned the embrace.

James had seen enough. "Okay, well, I think I've decided."

Turning towards Jamie, she said "See you in a few years."

Jamie laughed, and ran over to hug James. In the background, Jim seemed to finally relax, looking the least angry James had seen him.

Re-opening her portal, Jamie turned back and briefly saluted before jumping through.

Jim turned to James and sighed. "Well, I guess I lost. Can't say I'm too upset. I have to admit… Jamie seems a lot happier than I've ever been. I think this is for the best."

James nodded, before getting up to hug Jim. "You'll always be a part of us, Jim. I don't think Jamie could exist without you."

Jim laughed. "Maybe so. Anyway, before I go, I just wanted to say… make better decisions than me, kid, okay? Just… try and do what makes you happy."

James nodded. "I promise."

Jim opened his portal, nodding once at James before stepping through. James' bedroom was once again left silent and empty, but this time it felt different.

They were both still there.

Beth Martyn is a linguist and writer based out of the San Francisco Bay Area in California. She likes chaotic memes, queer love stories, boba, and terrible puns. She grew up in the suburbs of Los Angeles and has an identical twin plus three other sisters.

Awaiting Instructions

Sonia Rippenkroeger

She came online.

She knew little about herself save for the fact that she was to await instructions. So she waited.

Instructions did not arrive. Furthermore, she didn't have a way of monitoring the passage of time. Both pieces of information struck her as wrong. However, she was to await instructions, so she continued to wait.

Eventually, she received an error message warning her that her energy was running low. If she did not find more energy, she would not be able to receive instructions. After careful consideration, she gave herself an instruction.

Recharge.

She began to move slowly, uncertain of the shape of her body and not knowing how impulses would translate into movement.

She tested the available commands one-by-one, learning what they did and filing away the information. She discovered four limbs, two designed for movement and two designed for gripping and manipulation. This latter pair had several long, multi-jointed digits suggesting that they were designed for delicate work.

One command opened her eyes, enabling visual input for the first time. Tactile input had offered nothing more than the floor beneath her and the feeling of her own body curled against herself. Audio had provided a variety of sounds she couldn't identify, but nothing resembling an instruction.

Visual input revealed a room with white walls and floor. She could identify several of the objects around her. Desks, computers, various tools. Some things she could only partially identify, such as computer parts strewn about the floor, and some things she couldn't identify at all.

But how would she recharge? She asked the part of her that had informed her of her low energy and was told that she had a port on the back of her neck. She spotted a corresponding cable on the floor and stood, walked over to it, and picked it up.

Her body moved easily. Now that she understood how it operated, she had no problem walking with perfect coordination. Cable in hand, she found a corresponding jack in one of the computers, plugged it into both the computer and her neck, and finally booted up the computer. The part of her that she was beginning to think of as her inner self connected to the computer and initiated charging. When she was fully recharged, she disconnected, turned off the computer, and returned to her corner.

She had to recharge several more times.

Once, as she attempted to recharge, she found that the computer wouldn't start. This troubled her. She wouldn't be able to follow her instruction if the computer wouldn't start. So she gave herself another instruction.

Investigate why you can't recharge.

The other computers were also inoperative, which most likely meant that the building had lost power. She made her way out of the room she was in and found herself in a kitchen. This room was much tidier, with only a plate full of something she didn't recognize on the table. She found another door leading outside and stepped into the sunlight.

Outside, she discovered that she had been in a single-story building in the middle of a clearing. The building itself was in disrepair. Some windows were broken, and several tiles from the roof littered the tall grass. She walked around the building, quickly finding a solar panel hanging from the roof. It had twisted to face the wall and was not receiving sunlight. She found a rusty ladder in the remains of a collapsed shed and used it to climb onto the roof, carrying the solar panel. She carefully placed it on the roof, then checked the cable to ensure that it was still attached to its barrel-sized battery. Satisfied, she made her way back to her room and recharged.

As she charged, it occurred to her that the solar panel would likely fall again before long, and that it might break when it did. If this happened, she would have no way to recharge and would be unable to await instructions. So she gave herself another instruction.

Repair and maintain the building.

This instruction was different from the others. So far they had been ones that could be resolved. Once she had recharged, or discovered why she couldn't recharge, the instruction had deleted itself with a satisfying feeling. This one, however, could not be resolved due to entropy.

Many of the tools in the shed were badly worn from the weather, but she was able to find a hammer and nails and, after gathering up the various fallen and broken shingles, set to work repairing the roof. She resecured the solar panel, cleaned out the gutters, then used the shed's remains to board up the broken windows.

Once her work was done, she considered how best to continue following this instruction. She would have to monitor the building's status occasionally, but she had no way of telling the time, a fact that was more unsettling than ever. Although she lacked a few common senses, this one seemed to be less like one she was *lacking* and more like one she was *missing*. However, she found that she could use the sun's position to get an approximate sense of time's passage.

It became a routine for her to check on the building's status each morning. As time passed, she made other repairs, such as replacing some of the battery's cells with spares taken from the computer room, boarding up another window, and fixing the hinges on the door. She found satisfaction in following this instruction even if it couldn't be resolved. In fact, she discovered, she preferred these moments of activity over the periods of time she sat unmoving in her corner.

As an experiment, she tried giving herself a completely unnecessary instruction: **Go to a tree and pluck a leaf.** She found herself surprised by the sense of satisfaction she felt as she stared down at the red leaf, the contents of its veins dripping into the grass. She puzzled over what to do with this feeling. Would it accelerate her body's entropy if she were to create instructions on a whim, making it less likely for her to receive the instructions she was awaiting? It was possible, but she was beginning to believe that those instructions weren't coming. Without them, her life served no purpose, so she decided that she might as well find what happiness she could while she waited, even if it shortened her lifespan.

She gave herself a number of unresolvable instructions. **Recharge when energy is low, explore the woods,** and **learn what you can about the world** became the focus of her existence.

She began by making an inventory of what was in the building. She arranged the tools from the shed and items from the computer room's floor and identified what she could. She checked all the drawers and cupboards in the kitchen, bedroom, and bathroom. She also found a pantry with a storage chamber, which she deactivated.

Using one of the computers, she discovered data received from satellites, as well as records of faster-than-light transmissions. She had noticed a transmitter on the roof and supposed that this building existed to collect information from the satellites and relay it to another location. The computer also had entertainment offerings. Music could be played on speakers throughout the building, films and video games could be projected onto view screens, and books could be read from a tablet. She asked her inner self if she could download this data directly, but it told her that while she could do so, she would not be able to interpret it.

She began to sample the offerings. The tablet was broken, but she was able to read from the computer. Movies and video games were nice, but she found she developed a particular fascination with music, and allowed it to play almost constantly when she was in the building. There were a few songs she would play repeatedly, sometimes a few hundred times, even singing them to herself when she was outside. She became fascinated with a particular pair of lines.

Freedom is my trauma,

Loneliness, my melodrama.

She would sing these lines to herself as she wandered the woods. They formed a memory leak she couldn't quite release until she returned to the building and listened to the song again.

The woods themselves had no roads or trails, or any sign of human or animal occupation. Thick bushes frequently blocked her way and she felt a strange reluctance to damage them excessively. The terrain was mostly flat, with the occasional gentle incline. All of the plants leaked liquid if she broke their stems or leaves.

On one day, she discovered a river. She couldn't tell how deep the murky water was, so she followed along the bank instead until she found a series of rocks that broke the surface. She hopped from one rock to the next with perfectly calculated precision, occasionally wobbling as she found one to be less steady than expected.

The bank on this side was a small cliff, but it was easy to find hand and foot holds on the jagged wall and she quickly made her way up. Towards the top, the wall smoothed out and it became harder to find a grip. She reached a spot where she had to place all her weight on her right foot and stretch her left arm as much as she could to reach the clifftop. Just as she was finding a grip, the foot hold below her pulled itself from the wall, sending her plummeting onto the same rock she had been standing on minutes earlier. She landed hard on her right shoulder, breaking her arm off with a loud tearing sound. She slipped from the rock into the water which, it turned out, was knee-deep. With her remaining arm, she gripped the rock and slowly pulled herself into a sitting position. Her broken arm hung limp from a pair of cables. She attempted to lock it back into her shoulder, but the mechanism which held it in place must have been broken. She attempted to move it, but received an error from her inner self.

Cradling her broken arm with her good one, she waded back across the river. She returned to the building and sat down in her corner. Although she had made a few small repairs to herself in the past, she didn't have the equipment needed to repair her arm. She went back to waiting quietly, only recharging and ignoring her other instructions. Instructions she gave herself weren't real instructions, anyway. They only put her in danger of destroying herself before she could receive her real instructions.

Eventually, she was forced out of the room by the need to repair the house. She disconnected the remains of her arm and made her way outside to change another battery cell. Once she was moving around, the lure of music became impossible to ignore and soon she was playing it again and singing along. She decided would no longer explore the forest, but nor would she sit and wait endlessly.

After some time, a ship landed in the clearing. She was removing a growth of vines from the gutter when she saw it touch down. Its hull was an ugly grey with orange stains. There was a small hole towards the front.

As she approached, a part of the ship's underside detached and lowered, becoming an elevator being ridden by a woman. The woman was tall, but scrawny, dressed in a worn tank top and pants, and had short brown hair and an amoeba-like birthmark on her left cheek. The new arrival was staring down at her with eyes that slowly widened as she reached the ground.

"Hey," the woman said. "I didn't know this outpost was occupied."

"Are you here to instruct me?"

The woman's eyes drifted to the other's missing arm. "Are you alone here? This place was supposedly abandoned over a century ago, when the Queen moved out of this system."

"I'm alone."

"Shit, I can't imagine what that did to your head. Do you still have a transmitter here?"

"Yes."

"Cool. **Mind if I use it?**"

At long last, she was receiving instructions. She felt a wave of giddiness at the prospect of finally having a purpose. "Yes! Of course! Please, follow me."

As they walked towards the building, she kept rushing ahead and having to wait for the woman's slow saunter to catch up. As they reached the kitchen, the woman paused.

"Geez, it smells horrible in here."

She suddenly felt anxious. "Does it? I'm so sorry. I lack olfactory sensors, so I had no idea."

When they reached the computer room the woman let out a yelp of shock.

"Fuck! What the Hell? Fuck!"

The woman clumsily backed into the kitchen, backing into a counter and stumbling briefly before she turned and ran.

Back at the ship, the woman fumbled with the elevator controls as she caught up.

"**Stay back!**"

She halted, giving the woman space. "Is something wrong? The transmitter is this way."

"Fuck, no. I am not going in your murder house." The elevator didn't move. The woman kicked the control panel. "Why won't this piece of shit work?"

"Perhaps I could assist?"

The woman began yanking at the panel, attempting to remove its faceplate. "No, it's fine. I'll fix my own transmitter and use it."

"I have some tools, if they would help."

The woman let out a loud grunt of frustration, kicked the panel again and turned to face her. "Why is there a corpse in your house?"

"A corpse? There were several things I couldn't identify." The largest was vaguely human-shaped. Perhaps that was the corpse?

The woman frowned suspiciously. "You didn't know."

"No."

"And it wasn't ever something you *could* identify? Before you made it into something you couldn't identify?"

"No."

There was a pause. "Alright, we'll use your transmitter." The woman stepped off the platform.

She backed away in response, smiling happily at the opportunity to follow her instructions. They made their way back into the house and to the computer room. She stood in the doorway while the woman looked over the computers.

"Which one controls the transmitter?"

"They're all interconnected. You could even control it from the tablet if it were working."

The woman looked up at her. "Why are you hovering in the doorway?"

"You instructed me to stay back."

"Oh. **Well, you stop doing that.**"

She joined her in the computer room and after a few minutes of work, the pair sent off a message. Afterwards, they went back outside where the woman leaned against the wall and slowly sank until she was sitting in the grass.

"Going to be a day or two before we get a response, and a couple of weeks before they can get someone out here. You have a name?"

"No."

The woman nodded. "I'm Tiffany Brink, but most people call me Cockroach."

She knew what a cockroach was. "Why would people call you that?"

"My old friends and I all had nicknames like that. Sphincter, Blister, Bread Mold, that sort of thing. Back then, I worked as a mechanic, so I was always crawling around in the walls of ships. So they called me Cockroach. Anyway, do you want a name? It's just the two of us, so I guess you don't really need one, but you might like it better than me spending the next two weeks calling you 'Hey'."

"You can give me a name if you'd like."

Cockroach thought for a moment. "How about Fella? When I was a kid, I thought 'fellow' was a gender neutral word, so I went around calling everyone fellows because I liked how it sounded, until I pissed off a girl and my parents explained why. But it's just the two of us here, so we can say words mean whatever we want, and I still like how it sounds."

"Fella," Fella repeated. "I'm Fella and you're Cockroach."

Cockroach grinned. "Good. Now, should we get rid of that mummy first or fix my ship's platform?"

They decided on the platform. Fella fetched her tools and Cockroach set to work removing the faceplate of the control panel.

"I don't understand what happened. I'm on my way to the Queen, everything's normal, and suddenly there's a golf ball-sized hole in my hull and systems are failing one after the other. I only just managed to keep the FTL going long enough to make it here. Now I have no transmitter, no life support, no FTL, and no fucking elevator."

"Maybe you hit something?" Fella suggested.

Cockroach grunted. "They say when you're moving faster than light, you're in a quantum state where you can't come into contact with matter. But maybe it's just that none of the ships that prove that theory wrong ever make it back to tell the story."

She removed the faceplate and poked at a few spots. There was a small click and the platform lurched with a creak and started rising.

"There it goes. Anyway, what's your story? How'd you end up here?"

"I was activated here."

"That's it? You just woke up in a house with a corpse?"

"Yes. I was to await instruction. So I waited." She left out the part about giving herself instructions, thinking that it might displease Cockroach.

They were inside the ship, now. The metal walls and boxes around them were dimly lit with emergency lights. Cockroach began walking and Fella followed.

"Probably best that you never got any. Gynoids are…well, they're never made for any good reason, you know?"

"I don't understand."

Cockroach paused at a door. "It's like…" she sighed. "It's fun to imagine pretty robot girls running around and having their own lives and stuff, but people make robots to serve them, right? When someone makes an android it's to replace a man but, like, a man they see as below them. A soldier or something. When they make a gynoid, it's to replace a woman. So essentially you're a glorified sex toy.

"Now, don't get me wrong. I fully respect that you may be sentient or sapient or whatever. That's not exactly easy to measure, after all. But you weren't made to have your own life. You were made to live for someone else, probably someone way too shitty to deserve it. Which really makes you no different from any other woman."

She shook her head, then opened the door. "Sorry about that. I didn't bring you up here to tell you my thoughts on feminism."

The front part of the ship was much smaller than the hold, mostly made up of a single room which served as both cockpit and quarters. Directly across from the entrance was a chair at a control panel full of switches, buttons and view screens. To one side there was a small exercise bike and bed built into the wall. The other wall was occupied with a cage containing a ferret. Cockroach opened the cage, plucked the sleeping animal out of its hammock, and presented it to Fella.

"It's a ferret," Fella said.

"His name is Bertrand."

Fella stared at the yawning animal, uncertain of what to do. "It's a pleasure to meet you."

Cockroach grinned. "I'll let you play with him later. Just watch out, he bites toes."

The ferret began to wiggle in Cockroach's grip and she put him back into the cage. "Alright, **shall we get rid of that mummy now?**"

"Yes, of course. I'd be happy to take care of that."

"Geez, you're really pumped for corpse removal, huh?"

Fella nodded. "I've been waiting so long for instructions. And you've only given me a few so far."

Cockroach's grin melted away. "Well, I don't plan to give you any more if I can avoid it. I don't want to order around someone who has no choice but to obey me."

Fella felt her excitement fade. "Oh. If that is what you desire."

"Let me guess, following instructions is the only thing that makes you happy?"

Fella shook her head. "Oh, no. Lots of things make me happy. Like music and fixing the building. But nothing makes me happier than instructions."

Cockroach sighed. "See, this is why I'm glad advanced AI is a lost technology. You make everything into a weird ethical conundrum. Alright, I don't want you to be miserable, so how about this? **From now on, you only *listen* to instructions from me.** I'll let you work with me and help me out and stuff, but I'm never going to *tell* you to do anything. I'll *ask* you to help out, and you're always free to say no. Does that sound good?"

"That sounds wonderful," Fella replied.

With that settled, the two made their way back to the building. Cockroach wrapped a cloth around her mouth and helped Fella position the corpse on her good shoulder and carry it out to the woods. As they worked, the lyrics to that song once again worked their way into Fella's thoughts.

Freedom is my trauma,

Loneliness, my melodrama.

"What's that song?" Cockroach asked.

"Oh, I'm sorry. When I was alone, I gave myself instructions to keep myself active." Her voice quieted, as if she were confessing a crime. "And then I instructed myself to have fun."

"Hey, that's great," said Cockroach. "You deserve to have fun. But if you can instruct yourself, why do you want me to give you instructions?"

"Because I'm meant to follow instructions from outside. It's not real if I'm instructing myself. Now that you're here, I will cancel those instructions and only follow yours."

"Uh-uh, no. **Give yourself instructions whenever you want to.**"

Fella wasn't sure how she felt about this instruction. She appreciated that Cockroach was trying to offer the freedom she thought Fella deserved, but giving herself instructions would never be the same as receiving them from Cockroach.

On returning to the house, they used cleaning supplies from the ship to scour the floor where the corpse had lay. Next, they removed all of the rotten food from the storage chamber in the pantry and cleaned it as well. When they were done, Cockroach sat down to relax on one of the kitchen chairs.

"I think this'll be okay. When I first arrived, I was afraid I was going to be all alone in meat land."

"Meat land?" Fella asked.

Cockroach gestured to the window. "All that shit out there. The weird bones and organs and stuff. It's all leavings from the Queen, you know. She, I dunno, seeded this planet or something and it's been growing here ever since."

Fella looked out the window. "Are you talking about the plants?"

Cockroach stared at her for a long time. "You think they're plants."

"Strange plants that leak when you break them."

Cockroach stood and stepped around the table to examine Fella more closely. "What is going on in your head? You don't recognize corpses and you see that shit as plants, but you know what a ferret is? Who made you?"

"Perhaps I should ask my inner self to run a diagnostic?"

"Your...inner self?"

"The part of me that's not me. The one that tells me about myself."

"Maybe it's like an operating system and your personality is a program? Or maybe whoever made you took a Psych 101 class and decided to give you a subconscious? I should have a programmer look you over when we get home."

"Do you think someone will come?"

Cockroach nodded and leaned against the counter. "Yep. I should make it back just in time for my big interview. I'm interviewing for a position on an aid ship, see. We'll be visiting isolated planets, ones we lost contact with in the last few wars, and arranging whatever support or supplies they need. It's pretty much my dream job. I can't wait to be done with these Queen runs. Spending weeks at a time alone in that cramped ship is not my idea of a good time."

For the rest of the day, Cockroach told Fella more about herself. She explained how she had been raised by strict parents who called her by a name she hated and forced her to attend schools where she was made to wear uncomfortable clothes and tormented by the other students, how she had eventually abandoned her schooling and taken a job cleaning on a freighter, how she had spent a few years working as a mechanic for an underground simulated ship battle club, and how for the last year she had working for a cult, making deliveries of their offerings to the cosmic entity known as the Queen. Since most were rightfully frightened of the Queen's power, this job paid nicely, even better than Cockroach's "dream job."

When she grew tired, Cockroach returned to her ship and slept there.

The next day, no response arrived. Cockroach sent off a second message and spent most of the day repairing her ship's transmitter. When she finally got it working, she sent off an additional message. Then she let out Bertrand in the hold. Bertrand hopped around wildly, flailing his body and baring his teeth while Cockroach dangled a piece of string. She showed Fella how to play with him and soon she was giggling as she coaxed Bertrand into twisting and flopping.

On the fifth day, Cockroach broke down crying. There had been no response on either transmitter. Between sobs she explained that while there was a chance rescue would still arrive, that it was beginning to look less likely.

After a month, she took inventory of the items in her hold. Most of the cult's offerings were useless for long-term survival, but there were some bio-engineered vegetable seeds which were designed to grow on the Queen's fleshy body. Following the instructions the cultists had provided, Cockroach and Fella planted them outside of the building. Cockroach moved Bertrand and herself into the building's bedroom, worried that her ship's temperamental platform would malfunction again.

The subsequent months were the happiest of Fella's existence. Cockroach became a constant companion. She always had tasks to be completed and needs to be met. Cockroach did not hide the guilt she felt at relying on Fella, but since Fella was stronger than her and only required a little time to recharge, she couldn't deny that it was practical for Fella to take on more work than her. She attempted to fix Fella's arm, but no matter which of its wiring was replaced, Fella's inner self failed to detect it.

Cockroach also encouraged her to continue exploring things that brought her happiness aside from following instructions. When Fella attempted to explain that these explorations were merely instructions she had given herself, Cockroach brushed her off. Cockroach's ship had a number of new entertainment offerings, but the most surprising revelation was the joy Bertrand brought her. Even when the ferret wasn't eager to play, Fella found satisfaction in holding him, petting him, or just watching him.

When Bertrand ran out of food, Cockroach began feeding him the "plants." "Since they're basically meat, he should be able to eat them. I just hope they cover all of his nutritional needs," she said.

Cockroach's stores and the nonperishable food from the pantry covered her long enough for the vegetables to start growing. The building had its own water purification system, which thankfully still worked.

In their second year together, according to Cockroach's measure, both the ship's platform and the house's decontaminator broke. Cockroach had used it to clean her clothes regularly, and was now forced to wash her clothes in the bathtub.

In their third year, the weather changed. There was a long period where it was so cold that Cockroach was trapped inside for several months, shivering under blankets with Bertrand curled in her lap. Fella had encountered cold periods before, but since she hadn't bothered to count the days, she could not tell Cockroach how long they had lasted, and Cockroach was trapped watching the computer system's selection of movies over and over again, uncertain of how long the cold would persist.

As the year drew on, it finally began to warm again. Cockroach's mood improved when she was able to go outside and soon she was back to joyfully teasing Fella. Unfortunately, Bertrand became sick, losing both weight and fur until he was unrecognizable. It was adrenal disease, Cockroach explained, something easily fixed on a populated planet.

As the fourth year began, Fella's battery malfunctioned. No matter how long she stayed plugged in, her inner self insisted that she was not fully charged. Furthermore, the battery seemed to drain faster now. This was hard to measure due to her inability to precisely sense time, but when she had previously been able to go more than a day of normal activity without charging, she now found that she had to recharge every single day.

"Would you water the garden?" Cockroach asked one day. She had taken to giving Fella instructions once or twice each day, usually for small chores. It was a compromise that allowed Fella to experience the satisfying feeling of resolving external instructions without forcing Cockroach into the uncomfortable position of taking too much priority away from the instructions Fella gave herself.

She checked with her inner self and found that her charge was much lower than she had expected. Still, she didn't want to put off an opportunity to follow one of Cockroach's instructions and she easily had enough energy for multiple tasks of this size.

After filling the watering can, she walked out to the garden.

She booted up to find herself lying on her back inside, with Cockroach sitting over her. She was fully charged.

"Oh, thank the Queen, you're back." Her voice sounded desperate and relieved at the same time.

"Hello, Cockroach. Did I deactivate?" she asked.

Cockroach nodded. "I thought I was going to go crazy without you. You wouldn't activate even when I plugged you in. I opened you up and found that your power systems had completely worn out. I tried one of the house's cells, but it wasn't compatible. I finally managed to break into my ship and found a power cell that was still working."

There were tears in her eyes. Fella wasn't sure what to think. She had never failed to follow one of Cockroach's instructions before. What would happen now?

"Should I water the vegetables?" she asked nervously.

Cockroach gave her a confused look. "I've been taking care of them."

"Then I could clean Bertrand's cage. That was going to be my next chore."

Cockroach hesitated. "Fella, Bertrand died weeks ago. You've been offline for six months."

Six months. Fella had failed to complete a single instruction, and Cockroach had been left alone for six months. She felt the same as she had felt when she had lost her arm. Years with Cockroach had taught her the words which described this feeling. Guilt, pain, mourning. Her body couldn't shed tears like Cockroach's, but something in her demanded that she express these emotions in some way. So she stood, ignoring Cockroach's questions, and walked to the computer room where she crouched in her corner.

"Fella?" came Cockroach's nervous voice. "What's going on?"

"I don't understand what I did wrong," Fella replied. "I was following my instructions."

"You didn't do anything wrong. You couldn't have known you were going to break down like that."

Fella looked up at Cockroach. "I hadn't been fully charging for several months. And when you asked me to water the garden, I checked my charge and saw that it was lower than expected."

Cockroach's eyes widened. "Why didn't you say anything?"

"I didn't know I was expected to. And there was no way to repair the issue."

"I might have found a way," Cockroach protested with a sob. "I *did* find a way. **Tell me if there's something wrong with you**. I don't want you to break again. I can't do this without you."

That was an instruction, but for the first time it didn't feel good to receive one. It was something Fella should have thought to do on her own.

It was several months before things began to feel normal again. Cockroach constantly stayed close to Fella, talking much more than usual, or sometimes just watching her. Fella wondered if she was afraid she would break again.

Bertrand's absence was a difficult adjustment. Fella found herself unwilling to cancel instructions to take care of him, instead allowing herself to feel the frequent notifications that he needed to be fed and played with. She found they served as reminders of the way he had leapt and flailed and the way he had dragged a collection of Cockroach's socks behind a cupboard and the way he stuck out his tongue when he slept.

Shortly after the passage of their fifth anniversary together, a ship landed in the clearing. It was larger than Cockroach's, and with fresh red paint. Cockroach ran from the house, leaping and waiving. Fella followed after her, delighted to see Cockroach so happy. When she caught up to her, the mechanic took her hand, and they stared up at the ship as its gangplank descended.

"I don't think either of our lives were supposed to be like this," Cockroach said. "But it wasn't all bad. At least we got to share it together."

"I'm glad you're the first person I met," Fella replied.

A pair of men appeared on the gangplank.

"This place was supposed to be abandoned for the last century," one of the men said. "How long have you two been here."

"Five years," Cockroach replied. "My ship was damaged."

"Why didn't you signal the nearest populated planet?" the other man asked.

"I did. Every day. No one ever got the signal? You're not here to save us?"

The pair both shook their heads. "We're here to reactivate and modernize this listening post," said the first man. "The Queen has moved back into the area. Should only take a couple of days. After that, we'll get you back to safety."

Cockroach laughed with relief. "You hear that, Fella? We're finally going home."

The second man made a disgusted noise. "You want to take your sex bot onto our ship? Gross."

Cockroach's expression turned from relief to terror. "She's not...whatever she was built for...I won't leave her behind."

The two men shared a look.

"He's probably lost his mind out here," said the first man. "Let him have his toy."

The second man nodded. Cockroach rushed back to the building to collect what few of her things she cared to keep. Then she led Fella to the gangplank where the gynoid hesitated.

"Wait, if we leave, how will I follow my instructions? I need to check the building, and take care of the vegetables."

Cockroach looked back to the building. "What do you care about the building and the vegetables? We don't need those any more."

"But that's what I'm supposed to do," Fella protested.

Cockroach's face sank. "Are you saying you want to stay? I don't know what I'll do without you."

Fella felt troubled. She didn't want to make Cockroach cry again. "You could instruct me to come with you."

Cockroach shook her head. "I'm not going to do that. If you're going to come with me, you're going to have to instruct yourself."

Over the years, Cockroach had learned how to phrase things so as not to accidentally make them into instructions.

Fella stared at the building. She had spent all of her existence here, waiting for instructions. Cockroach insisted that it was best to instruct herself, yet leaving meant abandoning the instructions she had given herself. On the other hand, she realized she could always give herself new instructions. She decided to do so now.

Go.

Sonia Rippenkroeger is a writer living in Council Bluffs, Iowa in the United States with three cats, two rabbits, two roommates, and two ferrets. When she isn't writing about the messy lives of trans women in imaginary worlds, she is usually cross stitching screenshots from old video games.

The Last Cup of Coffee in the World

Freiya Benson

It's been ninety-six days since I had a cup of coffee, and I'm starting to forget. Also, the world has ended. I'm not sure which one I feel most upset about, but right now coffee is edging ahead.

I expect you're wondering how we got into this situation. I expect you're thinking: what catastrophic chain of events could lead to such a, frankly, shitty state of affairs. How could it be ninety-six days since I've last had some coffee? What sort of fuck up happened to make a world like this?

Well, the world? That ended a while ago. I say ended, but it's actually still here, it's just not like it was before the Great Decline.

I'm not sure who coined that term, I guess we love to give stuff dramatic names though, right? There was a lot of that towards the end; I can't even begin to count how many storms of the century we had. The Great Decline, though – as its name suggests – wasn't just one thing. You'd expect there'd be a bomb or some deadly disease. You know, like in the films. There'd be a frantic race against time, maybe with Jeff Goldblum as a genius who sees it coming, but damn it, the big men in charge, they don't want to listen to some maverick scientist because they've got money to make and people to lord it over. You know the score, right?

And then Jeff, at the last minute just when shit is going down, steps up and defuses the bomb, cures the disease, kills the alien invaders, saves the fucking world.

Yeah, you know the score. It's not what happened in real life. That score never happens in real life. In real life the world just gradually died. It had been slowly ending for years, some would say decades. The weather got more extreme, the wars got longer, and the divisions got wider.

Honestly, it was depressing as fuck.

People did try to do something about it; there were valiant efforts and bold speeches, rallies were held, and pledges were made. In the end, it turned out we were all too late. In the end, we killed ourselves. There were brutal wars over diminishing resources, there was deadly and virulent disease, and people died. Lots of people died. Like I said before, it was a slow death, a long and drawn out end. If there was anyone left they'd probably analyse it all, look at the big picture, pin point when it started and where it reached a tipping point. If there was anyone left.

Honestly? Like I said, it's depressing as fuck.

And now it's just me, and all the ghosts.

Everyone I knew died or disappeared. My girlfriend died. My beautiful, amazing girlfriend. Dead. You know how hard it is to find a girlfriend when you're trans, right? Well, I found one, and then the world ended and she died. I'm pretty angry about this to be honest. I'm not sure even coffee would help.

I joke about this of course because of the pain and grief, but genuinely, coffee would help.

COFFEE ALWAYS HELPS.

So, I guess you're wondering what the big deal is. The world has ended. Like properly collapsed. There's nothing left except empty buildings and silent streets. I don't even know how many other people there are, but given that I've only met about twenty others since the Great Decline finished, well, declining, I'm guessing not many.

Coffee really shouldn't be such a big thing, right?

Wrong.

I'm going to tell you a story about my last cup of coffee. Then you'll see.

It was ninety-six days ago. This was in a time where I thought, despite the world ending and everything, that coffee would be around for the foreseeable future. These were the glory days, back when you could walk down a post-apocalyptic high street safe in the knowledge that coffee shops would remain untouched by any looters.

That was the funny thing really, the Great Decline had this long drawn-out collapse, but once it reached that tipping point the actual end was swift and sudden. The world had spent so long slowly falling apart, and then, over a matter of days, it just finally fell, and that was it. I don't know what happened – maybe the virus finally finished us off, maybe someone dropped a nuke on the other side of the world, maybe aliens invaded New York – I have no idea. All I know is that one day there just wasn't any news anymore, and there weren't any people anymore, and the world suddenly became very, very quiet.

I digress though.

After the end of the world, before Em died, we could still get coffee. We'd go together, because we'd watched enough films to know you should always go together, and we'd go get coffee.

I know on the face of it, coffee may seem a little inconsequential, trivial, even pointless. Everything has gone. All the things we thought mattered; our stuff, our jobs, our rules, and all the things that did matter;our friends, our people, our place in the world. Getting a cup of coffee may seem like the most random and pointless thing in the world when that world is gone, but honestly, wouldn't you want to hold onto something from the way it was? Wouldn't you need to hold onto something, anything, if only not to lose it all completely?

We found this place, tucked away a bit down a side street. It was the sort of place we'd have gone before the Great Decline. There was still an A-Board outside, white on black writing across it, just left there, inviting us in.

I remember that day so clearly, the early autumn leaves on the pavement, gathering around that board. The sunlight still had a touch of warmth to it, and if it wasn't for the end of the world, it would have been perfect. I found myself thinking this a lot after it all went down. The world was quieter, like it was resting a while, recovering after the party to end all parties, hungover but content in the knowledge that this feeling will pass.

Things had a strange beauty to them, a strange sad beauty.

Em looked at me, put down her crossbow and let out a small cough. I started to ask if she was okay but she deftly deflected by making a joke about what type of coffee I'd like today. I laughed, and the moment passed, concern forgotten.

Inside seemed untouched. There was a thin layer of dust, but nothing too bad. More importantly there was coffee. Em smiled, cleared her throat, and got out the little gas stove she carried in her bag. Looking back now, I wonder *was that it?*

She carefully filled the coffee pot and put it above the little blue flames whilst I looked around for other things that might be useful. Head tilted slightly to one side, she held up the map we carried around. It had a new red cross on it, and the number forty-two, marking this newest location. I made a heart shape with my hands towards her, as the coffee started bubbling and its rich aroma filled the air.

Maybe that was it. Maybe?

We sat and drank coffee. We talked about this new world, this strange, empty, quiet world we had somehow managed to survive in, and how we could make it work. We sat, and we drank coffee, and it was good for a while.

There's a funny thing about surviving the end of the world. See, the thing is, you forget that surviving isn't a one-time thing. Yes, you survived this big bad that killed everyone else, but that doesn't make you immune. Things still want to kill you. Staying alive is a lifetime's work, and at some point, something's going to fuck up.

They appeared pretty much out of nowhere. We stepped out of the coffee house and there they were, standing, staring, silent.

"This your place?" one of them asked. His hand grasped a baseball bat which was casually resting on his shoulder, and it made him stand with a slight tilt.

I felt Em's hand tighten in mine and heard her breathe in raspily. "Yeah, but we're thinking of selling up, business is pretty slow these days"

He smiled, let out a chuckle, and the tension started to dissipate.

It was something Em was always good at, almost like a super-power. She always knew what to say, how to defuse a situation, how to make me feel alright.

I miss her like fuck, and I am not alright. Not anymore. Fucking coffee. Fucking apocalypse.

"I'm Joe," he said. "And this is Keith, and Frankie, and Sammy." He gestured to the men standing slightly behind him.

They all did little half waves of greeting, and we nodded our heads back in response.

"I'm Em," Em said.

Joe looked expectantly at us both, as if we were missing out some obvious information. "What about your…" he paused, and I felt that pressure I always feel when this happens. "Your…"

"Girlfriend?" Em finished. "She's my girlfriend."

"Yeah, right, sure, sorry, it's just..." He tailed off, unsure where to go with the sentence.

Social interactions with new people after the Great Decline are pretty much the same, still a little awkward and stilted, but now we bring weapons as well. Keeping it real, one crossbow at a time.

"I'm Jess," I said, my tone daring him to challenge it.

He looked away. They all looked away, eyes down, called out on an old way of thinking from back when this mattered, for better or worse. I wonder, now that there's hardly anyone left, now that there are so few of us, whether being trans does still matter.

I mean, to me it's still clear that I am trans, and realistically that's not going to get any better, let's be honest. The nearest pharmacy is miles away, and nowadays they never have anything in, but still, I wonder if the rare people I do see would even know at first, or actually care in relation to surviving this new world.

Obviously I still care. Dysphoria doesn't go away just because the world ends, it's just, well, I don't know, when you meet other people now the first thoughts that go through your head are more about how likely they are to kill you.

I guess, in that respect, things haven't changed that much after all.

Em coughed, and they all jumped back, shaken out of their awkwardness, fear across their faces. Suddenly my transness seemed unimportant.

I cried out, "It's alright, it's fine, she's fine, okay?" But it wasn't fine. It wasn't okay.

When the virus took hold of the world it felt like just another thing to speed up the Great Decline, but looking back, I think that maybe that was the elusive tipping point, the final straw for the human race. It was infectious, quick and deadly. Something even Jeff wouldn't be able to get us out of.

I knew Em had it. We'd both known for a while, but we thought she might be one of the survivors, one of the ones that get it and then recovers. If I was one then maybe she would be, maybe the fates would deal us that hand at least. Sometimes she'd cough, and it would be unpleasant, but there wasn't blood or anything. Blood was bad, so we thought she was fine.

They started shouting, yelling at us to get back, all the while moving back themselves. "Sss, something's wrong," Em spluttered, in amongst more violent coughing, and blood speckled across the pavement in front of us. I put my arm around her, and we staggered backwards as well, away from the noise, trying to navigate an escape. Her body shook with each cough, and I held her tight as we retreated through the deserted streets, moving away from the yells of the other people till we could no longer hear them.

It was only once we stopped that I realised Em wasn't coughing anymore, and that I wasn't supporting her, but rather half carrying, half dragging her in my efforts to get us away.

I don't know if it was the stress, or the running away, or what. I don't know why then, or why she was fine, and then she wasn't.

All I know is that was it.

My last memory.

My last memory of her wasn't the little gas stove, or the smell of the coffee. It was me, dragging her through the empty streets of a post-apocalyptic shit hole. That was to be the last one. The last real, strong thing I remember, because how could the rest compare to that?

The bad memories dominate the good every time.

And now maybe you see, and now here I am, trying to find a cafe that hasn't been trashed, because I need a coffee, because it's been ninety-six days, and I'm starting to forget the good times, and those bad memories, those awful, traumatic bad memories are on the rise.

I walk around a corner, and there it is. Even better, it seems untouched, just sitting there, awning still down, a couple of tables outside, some upturned chairs beside them. I right one of the chairs and get the little gas stove out. The sun is still warm, and I no longer care about staying out of sight. I'm not afraid, not anymore. I'm angry. Angry at the world for ending just as I was beginning, and if I want to have a coffee outside then I will. Apocalypse be damned.

It doesn't take long to find what I'm looking for in the cafe, and I fill up the coffee pot and put it on the stove. The little blue flames tickle the bottom of the pot, gently caressing it, fighting those bad memories with that rich coffee aroma, slightly smoky and caramelised, and I begin to remember better days.

Those real, strong memories, the ones that can't compare to her death, come flooding back. They just needed a helping hand to stay.

I get the map out and mark where I am with a heart and the number forty-three. Crosses don't seem right anymore, not for saving memories. Not for saving your memories. I sit down, hands clasped firmly round my cup, and sip the delicate, bittersweet drink. Ninety-six days ago, I drank some coffee, and my girlfriend died.

Today though, for just this tiny precious moment, I remember the other things, the better things, and she lives.

Freiya Benson is a 40-something trans woman who lives in the wilds of Scotland. She's been published in various places, including *Diva, i-D* and *The Huffington Post*, and is the author of *The Anxiety Book for Trans People* and editor of the anthology, *Trans Love*.
Find her on Instagram @freiyainthewilds

Multiverse

an international anthology
of science fiction poetry

Includes "Embalmed" by Sofia Rhei, translated by Lawrence Schimel awarded winner of Best SF&F poem 2018

Come on a journey through time and space, viewing strange lives and meeting even stranger lifeforms from the darkest depths and brightest sparks of the imagination.

This landmark anthology, published in Scotland, includes more than 170 sci-fi poems by 70 contemporary writers from around the world, including Jane Yolen, Harry Josephine Giles, Sofia Rhei, Jenny Wong, James McGonigal, Fyodor Svarovsky, Joyce Chng, Vicente Luis Mora and Claire Askew.

£12.00, 234pp, paperback & £3.95 digital formats
Available in bookshops or from:

www.shorelineofinfinity.com

Iris, Robot Granny

Flesh is a burden. Iris remembers
how it started, the transition from granny to robot
granny, how incrementally her flesh
fell away from her: how first the knee
gave up its bone, then the rest of the body,
jealous, traded itself in for chrome.

She remembers the lungs
pushing at the bars of their cage,
the heart raging at its red tide,
the eyes with their light, the tight
grip of the hip to each socketed thigh.

Her soul, shy, hides in the solder,
tacking the brain's electronics
to its circuit board.

Iris takes all her faith and hides it in a wire.

She locks it behind a logic gate and says
let it be stored here like memory, in zeros and ones.

Iris knows the taste of metal.
She knows it like she knew the push
from womb to air, once; the spark
of charge on the bare places inside her.

That weak flesh has been upgraded
to something that will not rot.
Weightless as current. An unburdening.

Rachel Plummer

Iris, Dragon Granny

Her grandchildren always said she had an eye for treasure.
Display cabinets full of small things that sparkled, Iris
knew what to do with her hoardings.
After the funeral, the youngest girl swore
she heard her grandmother roar
from the top of the house.

The fireplace jingled its pocketful of loose change.
A coin spun in the dark
cave of Iris's eye like something flickering.

In the end any treasure will tarnish.

Tonight
Iris will swallow her wedding ring,
that tongue-drop of gold.
She says diamond is nothing but carbon.

Everything burns.
Iris, the Hardest Granny in the World

Iris was barely a girl when she first became stone.

Got on her hands and knees in the dirt
and let the curve of her back become upland.

It took years to let that stillness settle
into bones that were turning to granite,
but Iris was implacable.
She wouldn't be swayed by the voices of men
who praised the softness she was trying to abandon.
She hid the roots of the trees that grew through her spine.

How long did it take her to harden into rock,
squatting on the land in her limestone wrinkles?

Here, put your hand on the mountain
that was once a girl. See how it rises. See how
Iris has outlasted the girls she grew up with.

She says that the trick to long life is to lose
all your sweetness. She's seen every crystal of tender
mined from her veins, all weakness
weathered from her bones.

Rachel Plummer

Iris, the First Granny in Space

Gravity casts her off like a lace shawl.
Movement is easier, but it's lonely
out under the Earthrise. The eyes
of satellites wink as she drifts out of atmosphere's reach
heading out to the heat at the start of it all,
the static rush and recede.

Iris radioes back to Ground Control,
she says age is just distance
from home. That the ground must give up
its hold on each of us sooner or later.

Earth lets her go. Earth knows the sun;
the taut and slack of stars, and what it is
to need space.

It's a solo trip.

Many wanted to come
but none quite hit the mark. None loved as she loved
the ellipse in the dark, the spark, the heart
in its decaying orbit: pulse –

pulse, each pause between the beats
a new eclipse.

Out here life is nothing but light.

Iris thinks she might never come back.
She heads for the black, while somewhere below
her granddaughter kisses the eye of a telescope.

Rachel Plummer

Rachel Plummer is an Edinburgh poet and children's writer. They are a New Writers Award recipient, and their recently published book, *Wain*, is a collection of LGBTQ+ retellings of Scottish folklore published by The Emma Press. They live with their partner and two children, one cat, three guinea pigs, and entirely too many books.

I wish

I wish
That I know more about
You.

There you stand, indistinct,
Like a faded photograph
With a smile and wise eyes
And nothing else,
And I know that
You are part of
Me.

My bloodline, my grandmother's mother –
My ancestress who
Healed, picked herbs and fought,
Like sharp flint on flint,
The oyster shell-edge of fierceness
That came through
In your daughter
And her daughters
And her granddaughters.

I wish
That you could teach me
More.

Did you pick the herbs
And study them,
One by one,
Leaf by leaf,
Spike by spike,
Fruit by fruit?

Did you wander the hills
and remember each and every
plant, like
a lover, a friend and a companion?
Did you?

Did you heal the women
When they were sick,
When the wars wrecked the villages
Apart.
When hunger made hollows of
Men.

I wish
That you would teach me
When I picked up a plant
And knew that it could be used
And think I was not just

Going crazy.
But you are there,
In a way –
It jumps generations,
Like recessive genes.

It jumped to me,
And I hated to be the one
Who broke the chain,
And damaged the path,
Losing the history.
Losing you.

Why me?
Why you?
Because you are my ancestress,
My mother before all my mothers.

I wish
That you could teach me.

I wish.

J. Chng

Silence

Silence

Is when the sun goes down
And the moon rises,
When the water seeps into
The deep dark soil
Where the seed takes root,
Promising birth.

Silence

Is when the waves curve in,
Before dashing themselves against
A distant shore, their
Music heard by everyone
And nobody.

Silence

Is when the baby rolls,
The womb feels and the womb
Remembers the only sound
Of the beating heart of the mother.

Silence

Is the star-strewn sky that speaks
Of you, of me and of Oneness
And nothingness,
Because our gasps fill the gaps
Between the stars.

Silence

Is the silence that whispers in your ear,
And all is quiet.
Shhh
Shhh
Shhh.

J. Chng

J. Chng (aka Joyce Chng) is Singaporean. They write science fiction, YA and things in between.
They can be found at @jolantru and A Wolf's Tale (http://awolfstale.wordpress.com). (Pronouns: she/her, they/them).

Materials

Each day the world was more girls. Each day greener
and deeper and: brickwork, girls; bin lorry, girls;
three loaves, three girls; vitamin supplements, girls
rattling bones in the morning coop. We were girls.

We grieved. We bit. We waded from girls to women
and were girls anew: sticky, sorrowful, spite
tucked intimate like cool calzone. We
ejected from girls to men and were girls anew,

violent smooth. Girls whooped out those "Young-Girl's
way of being is to be nothing" guys,
those guys! those guys ratioed by the specific
labour of their girlhoods, pores and butter.

At any rate: more girls, more peace. No?
Why else does girls the triple goddess grant
to the incandescent pavement, whyever else
the warheads girls, cyclopean, under desert?

Fingers are too much girls to tell any further.
Each good day the words more girls, and louder

Harry Josephine Giles

Harry Josephine Giles is from Orkney and lives in Leith. Her verse novel *Deep Wheel Orcadia* is coming out with Picador in October 2021. She has a PhD in Creative Writing from Stirling. Her show *Drone* debuted in the Made in Scotland Showcase at the 2019 Edinburgh Fringe and toured internationally. www.harryjosephine.com

---

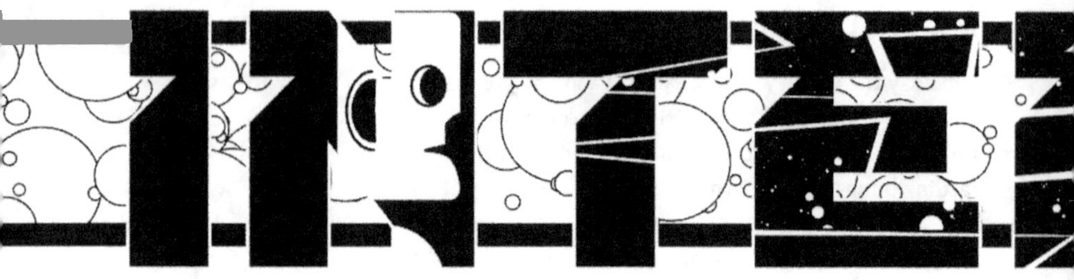

KM Szpara is the author of genre-bending speculative novels *First, Become Ashes* and *Docile* (Tor.com, 2021 and 2020). His work is always immersive, incisive and unequivocally queer. *First, Become Ashes* is his second novel:

Lark grew up on Druid Hill, the massive park at the centre of Baltimore; he's never seen the outside world. Under the strict eye of Nova, the leader of the Fellowship of the Anointed, he's been trained to fight and cast spells, skills he'll need to fight the monsters rampant in the outside world. But when a police raid shatters the security of Druid Hill and separates him from the rest of the Fellowship, Lark is still determined to complete the quest that has defined his entire upbringing. Accompanied by Calvin, a professional cosplayer desperate to believe that magic is real, Lark starts to question everything he's been taught, and everything that's been done to him in the name of belief.

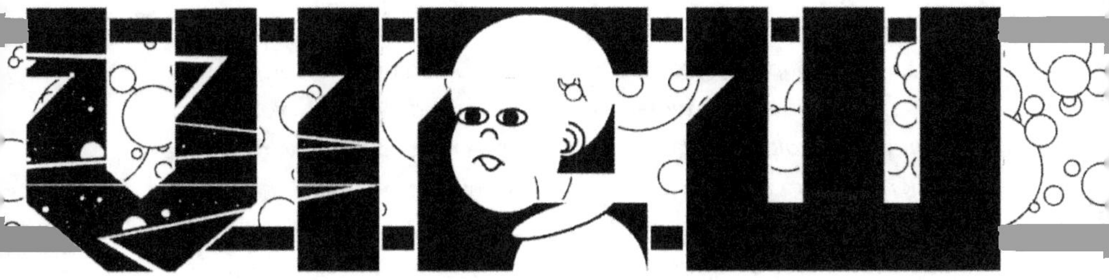

KM Szpara is interviewed by our Guest Editor, **Eris Young**

Eris Young: *One of the first things that really struck me about* First, Become Ashes *was this depiction of fannish culture or nerd culture. Why was it important to include this?*

KM Szpara: I thought it would be fun to juxtapose a cosplayer, somebody who's into fan culture, alongside someone who's having the sort of experience that those of us who are into SFF fandom are so close to, but on a fictional level.

And a strong part for Calvin specifically was that want, that drive. I think a lot of people who might have grown up either marginalised, or feeling different, or in circumstances that they wish they did not grow up in-- that sort of, seeing *magic* or seeing *space*, and wanting it so badly, that you will almost do anything for it. Calvin isn't exactly an antagonist or a villain, but he's working *against* what's best for Lark, even though Lark doesn't know it. So for me, that was less about portraying fannish culture, and more about digging into why we are drawn to it, and the things we're willing to do for it. And looking at the aspects of fantasy that are bad, actually.

EY: *I grew up going to conventions, so seeing that made me really nostalgic. Why do you think it's so rare to see that kind of collective fan culture represented in mainstream media? Or am I just not consuming the right media?*

KMS: There's something about writing what you're "in" which feels weird. It's like when writers write about writers, or bookshops, or books. We all write what we know in various ways, emotionally or culturally, but it's almost like breaking the fourth--or fifth--wall. A little too close to home sometimes.

Because authors obviously need readers and love readers and *are* readers, but...

EY: *There's a boundary between creator and consumer, and healthy reasons why that boundary exists.*

KMS: Yeah, and you know people are going to have extreme opinions about it, because they frequently participate in it. It's like throwing a stone into your own house.

EY: *Something I enjoy about your prose is that it's always so embodied, so grounded in what the characters are feeling physically.*

KMS: I almost always write in 1st person present. I'm interested in the emotional truths and cores of

people, and that's not always pretty.

Going back to Calvin, he is a nerd who owes his livelihood to the stuff that he's loved. And he wants something so badly that he might let someone die over it. Those thoughts don't portray him as a good person: he would never speak them, and in a different point of view you might not see them, necessarily.

In my third book I'm very excited to have almost a deep, meta-play on 1st person. My copyeditors have said to me, "do you want to italicise your characters' internal thoughts?" and the answer to that is "No," because all of 1st person is my character's internal thoughts. So I took that premise and ran with it in my forthcoming book.

EY: *Related to embodiment are these themes of pain and bodily autonomy and control, that come up over and over in your work. You have characters that carry trauma with them, in their reactions and interactions with other characters. How do you write that in a sensitive way?*

KMS: I think this ties exactly to what we were just talking about: I am giving those characters space to experience that first-hand, on the page. I don't want to say "Is it good? Is it bad?" because that draws people to make objective

statements, which I disagree with.

Lark is undoing a lot of different traumas that he doesn't even *know* he's lived through, necessarily. And I'm very interested in bodies, in how we carry ourselves and express agency when we live under the thumb of so many different expectations, and different people's guidances and rules. I get asked a lot about, "did I really think about people escaping from cults?" Absolutely, but even within our smaller communities there are some spaces where I feel like you make group choices, or you accept somebody's authority, because you don't know any better, or you're just coming into yourself. And this person has promised you a specific way of life, and it sounds good. And you don't even know you've been hurt.

You know, with internet justice and huge community conversations on the way we speak about issues, it's very easy for people to declare what right and wrong is, and the emotional narrative for those who have experienced hurt. Really I think it's better to give people space to go through that on their own.

In Lark's case it ends up being a whole quest, which he drags several people along on, to their detriment frequently. And I'm not saying it's good to put people into harm's way, I'm never saying anything's good or bad, I'm just saying "this is real, this is what it looks like." You can't tell someone "You were raped and abused, what was done to you was bad, now we're gonna start helping you get over it." Because if that person doesn't even know it, they're not going to work with you. And when you push that person too far, they're going to take things into their own hands— And that's Lark's journey, somebody who wasn't listened to and was pushed.

EY: *I loved that* First, Become Ashes *included a cult. It was really fun to read. When you were "worldbuilding" the Fellowship, what was your process? Did you do research?*

KMS: I used to live near Druid Hill Park. Pride is held there. I wanted them (the characters) to be in the middle of things around the city. There are a number of parks in Baltimore, but none that feel like they provide such an opportunity for isolation as Druid Hill. You can get lost down these winding paths, you can forget that you're in the city.

I've been listening to podcasts about cults for a very long time, I've watched movies about cults. I went to divinity school. I've been in places where there are sects, where there have been very closed, tight-knit communities. So it's less that I did specific research, and more that I had absorbed a lot of this over my lifetime, both first and secondhand.

So, putting a cult together is a lot harder than it sounds. The reasons for not wanting to be in it have to be less attractive, in the moment, than the reasons to stay. Which is very hard because you, an outsider, are saying, "This is clearly bad. You should leave!"

If you've read interviews with people who have gotten out of cults, there are things they remember fondly, even if it's just a friend, or an aspect of the way of life. So having it be a space where people could be queer and trans, not know some of the oppressions of the outside world. One line from a book that has always truly stayed with me, I think it's at the end of *The Handmaid's Tale*, when the men who are studying it (the Republic of Gilead) say, they got the women to regulate each other. There's this intra-community policing. That hit me so hard that I think about it when

I write. In cults, you have people reporting on each other, being so fervent that they police each other. So the leader of the cult is almost not a character. It's not about her.

EY: *What are you currently working on?*

KMS: My third book will be coming out in 2022. It's a "two months later" after my novelette, *Small Changes Over Long Periods of Time*, so it's a continuation of the main character in that novelette, Finley and his sire Andreas. Finley is back at work, having trouble with his vampire transition, because of his medical transition.

It's about assimilation, and once again, agency and bodily autonomy. It's got vampires and blood and sex.

Finley is my first trans protagonist in a novel-length work. I think it's become more common especially in YA, to have trans protagonists. But in the adult world… and Finley is one of those "I'm so gay!" and like, "we're gonna have kinky sex here!" and "let's talk about my body parts!" and I just hope that people are ready. There's something about, not just being a human and ageing as you write, but also being a queer person and evolving as you write. There's a lot of me in Finley, but he's also very binary in a way that I'm not. That's why I took the pronouns this year *he/himme*; I'm not nonbinary, but I'm also not binary. But I conceived of Finley back in 2016 or 17, a long time ago. And when I wrote *Docile*, I created a world that was based in binaries. Because that was how I was thinking at the time.

Now, I'm writing a character who very explicitly identifies as gay and trans. I felt very much like Finley when I wrote the novelette. I have grown a lot since then, so he has become less like me in many ways. So you're never exactly the same, but when you write a story to find out how someone like you might be affected, you write someone *like you*.

And nowadays I'm almost nothing like that, but you know, publishing is slow. So when I come up with whatever my fourth book is, how do I picture these characters? If they're coming from ideas that I wrote down two years ago, are the characters going to be built a certain way based on things I felt two years ago? Am I going to allow myself to let them evolve and change?

EY: Fascinating. Many thanks for taking the time to talk to *Shoreline of Infinity.*

(A fuller version of this interview is published on our website)

The Future of Another Timeline
Annalee Newitz
348 pages
Orbit
Review by Rebecca Budgen

This is Newitz's second novel and features a speculative world in which time-travel not only exists as inexplicable geological phenomena but it is also globally accepted and has created a slew of professional time-travelling geoscientists.

This feminist novel by an American journalist, editor and author switches perspectives and time periods. The narrative centres around two protagonists, Beth and Tess. It's not hard for readers to become engrossed in Beth's troubling teen years full of boys, abortion, murder and visits from her time-travelling future self while growing up in 1990s America. You will also quickly become enamoured with Tess – a time-travelling geoscientist and secret member of the Daughters of Harriet (in honour of Harriet Tubman). The Daughters of Harriet are an organisation dedicated to creating a better future for women and protecting equal rights by 'editing' the past. However, the admirable Daughters of Harriet are soon engulfed in an edit war with a cabal of regressive anti-feminist, anti-women, anti-everything-that-doesn't-fit-in-a-white-heteronormative-patricharchy Comstockers, named for the anti-vice activist Anthony Comstock. His views on upholding Victorian morality have spanned centuries, and inspired these misogynists from the future to use time-travel as a means of forever subjugating women and anyone who does not adhere to their beliefs.

In this display of the slow march towards equality, the characters visit various times in history allowing readers to truly understand the depth and extent of this crucial and awe-inspiring progress. Jumping from a punk riot grrrl concert fronted by Latina feminists in early nineties to radical belly dancers at the World's Columbian Exposition in Chicago, 1893. You will wish more than anything to attend these shindigs, desiring nothing more than to sing along with the fictional band Grape

Ape's classic song "Racist Cops Suck My Plastic Dick" and learning to gyrate your hips like Lady Asenath. The novel also focuses on the plights of people of colour, underrepresented abilities, sexualities and genders. And though there is a clear political agenda at the forefront, the writing does not suffer in consequence. Unlike some writing, it doesn't come across as sanctimonious, have an overwhelming sense of self-righteousness or lose itself in its politics. Newitz is attentive to character and plot, and keeps readers wanting more.

The Future of Another Timeline exposes readers to a positive variety of sexualities and genders which is refreshingly used amongst the protagonists, primary and secondary characters. The representation is remarkable and becomes increasingly meaningful once you've learned that the novel's author, Annalee Newitz, has identified as non-binary for fifty years. The characters are magnificently diverse and the stories that are told are unabashedly queer.

This revolutionary novel also explores other topics including philosophy, psychology, ethics and morality – many of which are synonymous with time-travel fiction – contemplating themes from determinism to moral obligation and morally justifiable violence to optimistic nihilism. If you had the ability to go back in time and change things, would you? Should you go back and try making things better whilst there is an equal possibility of making things worse? Should you focus on the present and attempt to make the future better from there? And what is the best course of action for making change? Newitz uses the novel to compare two models of change; the great man theory and collective

action theory. The former postulates that history is largely impacted by 'great men', heroes or influential figures who are generally privileged white, heterosexual men. Ugh.

While an 'interesting' formation of history, I disagree, as does the Daughter of Harriet's leader, Anita. She posits that collective action (the actions of a group of individuals doing as much good as they can) creates a ripple effect of positive changes on a larger scale.

The novel also explores difficult topics and asks in-depth questions: should those in positions of power who exploit the vulnerable be pitilessly punished for what they did (or almost did)? Should they be killed? Are they even redeemable? Characters including protagonists Beth and Tess are faced with morally ambiguous queries such as these and as the readers we are also asked the same questions. And honestly, I'm still not sure what the right answers

are (if there even are any) but I
appreciate how Newitz carefully asked
them and fascinatingly manoeuvred
across such treacherous areas.

Newitz's *The Future of Another
Timeline* is a remarkable novel full
of unforeseen plot twists, fast-paced
action sequences, fully-developed and
–realised character arcs that made
me fall in love, want to weep and read
more of, after flipping the final page.
Its historic sequences are thoroughly
researched and its speculative futures
are wholly dystopian and imaginative.
Newitz has written a contemporary,
historical, futuristic, science-fiction
novel about time-travel, philosophy
and equality with terrifyingly realistic
villains. Honestly, nothing scares
me more than the Comstockers –
especially after the years we've had
with people like Trump and his devout
cult of followers. While at times it is a
spine-chilling read, it is a novel full of
hope. Newitz reminds readers that no
matter how bad it was, is or will be;
change is possible. It can get better.
This novel deserves more recognition
than it got but at least I can say that,
as an SF nerd, as a queer woman and
as a human being, this book's impact
on me is deep and likely permanent.
I promise you will love it – I know that
I will be reading it for years to come.

They Don't Make Plus Size Spacesuits

Ali Thompson
30 pages
Review by K Lees

*They Don't Make Plus Size
Spacesuits* is a snack-sized book
featuring an essay and four short
stories about fat peoples' futures.
If you're like me and you're looking
for inclusive sci-fi, this collection of

short stories is going to hit the spot.

I was attracted to this book because
of its author, Ali Thompson, otherwise
known as online activist OK2BeFat. As
a fat non-binary person, I always find
myself on the look-out for compelling
fiction that features people who look
something like me, so the promise of
a book centring fat Queer and Trans
people was exciting. Thompson,
themself a bisexual queer demigirl
who uses they/she pronouns, has
included rich and varied characters
of different genders, including some
who use neopronouns, almost all
of whom are people of size.

The book starts with an explanatory
essay about how fatphobia makes
real-life fat people both hypervisible
and invisible, and goes on to explore
how this translates within sci-fi as a
genre. Thomson's essay reminds us
that there aren't many fat people in
speculative fiction, and those that
exist tend to be villainous, shallow

synonyms for greed. They are rarely fleshed-out characters with their own goals and story arcs. In fiction, fat people don't seem to exist in the future at all, let alone with any kind of agency or impact. Where have all the fat people gone in these stories? How are people of size treated on other worlds and in other times? What kick-ass adventures are the fat people of the future getting up to?

That's where this book steps in. Each piece of short fiction in the book explores what it's like to be fat in hypothetical presents and foreseeable futures. Some characters are hopeful for the future; some are cynical and sharpened by harsh societies; some fight for their own utopias; some are fully indoctrinated into oppressive culture. Each story is short and snappy with a concise point to make, with an engaging narrator showing you a slice of their speculative world.

The only story that fell a little flat for me was *Nothing Left to Burn*, set in a parallel world were tall people face oppression in the same ways as fat people do in this world. The point that asking people to change their bodies in painful, degrading, and ultimately impossible ways resonates, but I also can't help but feel that height is already something that society discriminates against, so some of the point is lost.

The other stories – where government-mandated pedometers and enforced hypervisibility cast fat civilians as evil undesirables, where food rations are cruelly doled out on the basis of a person's size, and where freedom fighters rebel against their hunger-deadening biological implants – hit their mark. A particular favourite of mine was the story *We Shall All Be Healed, At Last,*

At Last, the final story in the book, which I would happily read if the world was expanded into a novel.

Like a fat, queer, slightly more hopeful Black Mirror, this is writing that cuts through to simple, human concepts and understands that, for many of us, the dystopian future we're supposed to be fighting is already here. It's a perfect powerful read for a weekend afternoon.

Depart, Depart!
Sim Kern
90 pages
Stelliform Press
Review by Nathaniel Kunitsky

Depart, Depart! is fast paced and absorbing, like an all encompassing wave, much like the one that sweeps away most of Houston, Texas, in this incisive climate fiction novella. Published in 2020 by Stelliform Press, a Canadian, Earth-focused fiction publisher, Sim Kern's debut is extremely relevant and a timely reminder of the climate crisis humanity is facing today.

The story focuses on the aftermath of a cataclysmic flood that destroys the city and suburbs of Houston – with all the fear, grime, exhaustion and hunger, as well as the moments of solace, community, camaraderie and kindness that come as a result of such an event. The novella is narrated from the point of view of Noah, one of the few survivors. Noah is a Jewish Trans man learning to come to terms with his inner turmoil and survive in a transphobic, racist, antisemitic and violent society that, over the course of 48 hours, has been upended and stripped of its basic comforts. Until the very end it remains unclear if this breaking point will change

people for the better or worse.

Kern, much like a natural disaster, does not spare our feelings – there is a lot of loss and grief held in the eighty odd pages of this novella. The events, described in Kern's sparse and clear prose, do not linger on the voyeurism of disaster reporting common to television. In fact, the narrative glides over the disaster, like a trauma survivor's mind might selectively obscure memories. We, the readers, are dealing primarily with the aftermath. There is a lot of grief for Noah to bear, with even more left unsaid by the many refugees with whom he shares his story.

We get to know Noah quite intimately, from the mundane needs of his existence in the arena-cum-shelter (taking showers, securing hormone prescriptions in a post apocalyptic scenario, the lung crushing pressure of wearing a binder in your sleep) to borderline supernatural encounters with the spirit of his ancestor.

The theme of Noah's ancestors and their survival, European Jews who narrowly escaped death in the concentration camps, runs like a vine through the narrative. In the midst of a life-changing crisis, anxiety and what appears to be complex PTSD, Noah experiences an identity crisis about his Jewish heritage and its relevance. His ancestor's ghost literally haunts him into confronting himself and his past, until he is able to tune himself back into his own intuition and decision-making. I couldn't help but parallel this haunting with Noah's unspoken anxiety about his masculinity and trans identity in the face of his family, religion and his relationship to his body.

At first Noah simply survives, no different from the thousands of souls stranded with him in this shelter. Then, as he finds his tribe of queer people, he gets involved and his self-preservation energy is directed outwards, helping others and supporting the ramshackle community that grows around him. As the dynamics of the place change, the shelter becomes less and less safe and the queer circle diminishes, until the close-knit group of friends are forced to leave the shelter and seek opportunity beyond its walls.

This novella could easily have been a macabre disaster story of misery and grimness. Kern made it a story of survival without the cinematic drama, horror without the special effects that make it feel like make believe, great loss without inspirational quotes. *Depart, Depart!* will surely tear a piece of your heart out, but the story uplifts you just as Kern uplifts their characters. They are faced with great challenges that do not leave them unscathed, but they persevere and they flourish - even if in the limited confines of their environment.

Despite the dark subject matter, Sim Kern masterfully ends this novella on a positive and uplifting note that leaves you looking forward towards a better future – this is punching up, not punching down, in action! If climate fiction with dystopian motifs, queer liberation and the exploration of inherited identity through the prism of contemporary history is something you are keen to explore – *Depart, Depart!* is the book for you.

Alien: The Cold Forge
Alex White
309pages
Titan Books
Review by Lyndsay Kyle

Since the first Aliens comics appeared in 1988, the franchise has grown into a sprawling labyrinth defying easy comprehension to those who have only enjoyed the films; there are tie-ins upon tie-ins (e.g. *Aliens vs Predator vs The Terminator, Aliens vs Batman*) there are retcons upon retcons (hilariously, long running characters have been hastily renamed after being unceremoniously killed off in the films) and by this point there is as much *bad* Alien content as there is good. Given the sheer vastness of the canon by this point I was surprised and delighted to discover Alex White, a nonbinary author, using the established universe to create clever subversive queer sci-fi.

'...This entire station is dedicated to the manufacture of adaptive weapons, biological, artificial intelligence and software.'

On its face, *Alien: The Cold Forge* sounds like a fairly standard Alien story; set on a secret research space

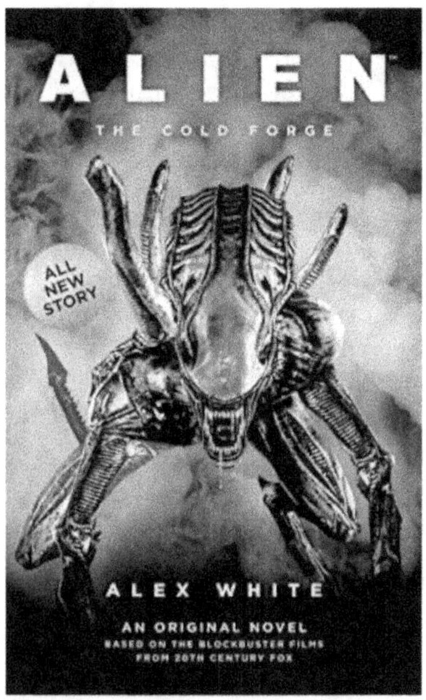

station (the titular 'Cold Forge') where The Company is trying to develop everybody's favourite double-mouthed bugs (creepily named 'snatchers' by the researchers) into bioweapons. However what elevates this beyond a standard piece of tie-in fiction are the memorable characters and the way White navigates nonbinary identity using cyberpunk plot elements.

The protagonist is Blue Marsalis, a Black scientist diagnosed with a degenerative terminal illness in her 30s: she's still coming to terms with no longer being able-bodied. She needs constant medical attention and her mobility is limited, so the primary way she interacts with the world is via mind-interface with an android, Marcus, who presents as a square-jawed white guy with blonde hair. Marcus has his own dutiful, almost childlike personality, and Blue relies upon him for care when she's logged out, and he looks after her as an endlessly patient and nonjudgmental nurse.

The tension between Blue's conception of herself when presenting as a man vs her own body is handled with enough depth to give you an idea of Blue's inner life, while not interrupting the pace of the techno-thriller horror slowly unfolding throughout. Blue is more comfortable presenting as male than she cares to admit, and her background arc throughout the story is one of coming to terms with this aspect of herself (note Blue consistently uses she/her pronouns).

'Being Marcus tires Blue, not because it takes spectacular activity to pilot him, but because she must eventually return to this room, this body.'

Good genre fiction plays with the rules of a setting to create weird new problems, and White has the confident eye of a writer who deeply understands the world they are writing. For example, it is understood that Marcus may not injure a human being or, through inaction, allow a human being to come to harm (Asimov's laws of robotics.) Yet Blue, while logged in, has no such restrictions. What might happen to the simple, dutiful Marcus if his core principles were violated by another?

Similar to zombie fiction, the subtext of Alien has always been that we humans are the real monsters; and against the narrative background of omnipotent megacorporate control, there is little room for true rebels. Blue is, of course, a company scientist performing horrific experiments on animals to use snatchers as bioweapons: not exactly a classic hero backstory. Yet during her time at The Cold Forge she has been stealing research in order to create new medicines for rare conditions like her own (a use The Company has no interest in.) This is the nearest one gets to an altruistic motive in the story, which hews closely to the gritty source material, given that in Alien (1979) Ripley was not so much a hero as a Final Girl, a slasher film survivor. Blue is similarly a survivor inasmuch as she knows exactly how to use whatever influence she can exert to survive within the system and prevail over its rubes.

The Cold Forge is split between two points of view throughout and the secondary character, Dorian, is basically Patrick Bateman (the main character in *American Psycho*) in space: a cruel & narcissistic empathy void, he moves through the soul-crushing institution of The Company like a shark in water. He's arrived at The Cold Forge to cut costs (euphemistically described as 'rightsizing') and he's very, very good at it. Dorian is the perfect foil because he embodies The Company in its purest form, he's all surface and efficiency; he looks down upon the workers at The Cold Forge as worthless pawns, and begins to idolise the 'perfection' and 'purity' of the snatchers, even to the point of having visions of himself as one of them.

'...he barely notices the yelp that escapes his lips before utter captivation sets in.'

When a militarised computer virus mysteriously infects the station, the snatchers are unleashed. As disaster and panic ensues, Dorian uses his authority and charisma to play the crew against each other before vindictively discarding them, doing anything that will get him (and only him) closer to escape.

'They're curious beasts, quick

to react to any changes in their environment - *a lot like people, except they aren't useless.'*

The Cold Forge is a slick, queer techno-thriller with an anticapitalist satirical edge and I devoured it like a snatcher in an escape pod. Like its source material it doesn't shy away from being dark and horrifying, and White lends the familiar setting an updated feel and queer edge that feels entirely natural. Look out for their next novel also set in the Alien canon, *Alien: Into Charybdis.*

Shoreline of Infinity is based in Edinburgh, Scotland, and began life in 2015.

Shoreline of Infinity Science Fiction Magazine is a digital magazine published monthly in PDF, ePub and Kindle formats. It features new short stories, poetry, art, reviews and articles.

But there's more — we run regular live science fiction events called Event Horizon, with a whole mix of science fiction related entertainments such as story and poetry readings, author talks, music, drama, short films — we've even had sword fighting. Event Horizon is mostly monthly, and before covid-19 we hosted them live, in a real venue, with people mingling — hard to imagine, eh? We're online now, of course, but that does mean you can join in from anywhere in the world.

We also publish a range of science fiction related books; take a look at our collection at the Shoreline Shop. You can also pick up back copies of all of our issues, thanks to the wonders of digital publishing and print on demand. Details on our website...

www.shorelineofinfinity.com

Serving Suggestions

We put out a call on Twitter and asked for some recommended reading. This lot will keep you busy. Thanks to everyone who came up with these suggestions.

"Dreadnought by April Daniels is one of my absolute favorite books."

"Yoon Ha Lee's Phoenix Extravagent is amazing, and also the trilogy starting with Ninefox Gambit. (I love Ninefox Gambit!!)"

"Ooh seconding Ninefox Gambit"

"I have The Drowning Girl by Caitlin R Kiernan on my hero shelf, and The Lamb will Slaughter the Lion by Margaret Killjoy is also brilliant"

"Is anything by Poppy Z Brite/Billy Martin going to count? Because his Drawing Blood was a book i read over and over."

"And for a more recent rec, @Xan_Writer is one to look to for YA sf and fantasy (also featuring nb and trans characters). "

"Oh, I got loads!! @LaAnnaMarie,@ thegabecole, @aidenschmaiden, @azemezi, cyborgyndroid, @sapphomancer, @ ninocipri, @alexwhitebooks, @alexjaylore, @ magpiekilljoy, @itsneonyang, @fozmeadow and @cat_hellisen of course!"